U0084729

序 言

　　本公司繼出版「初級英檢模擬試題①②③」之後，再推出「**初級英語口說能力測驗**」，完全仿照「初級英語檢定測驗」第二階段的複試測驗，題型包括複誦、朗讀句子與短文，以及回答問題，希望能幫助已經通過初級檢定初試的讀者，輕鬆通過複試測驗。

　　許多人通過了「初級英語檢定測驗」初試，但是對於即將面臨的複試，心存不安，原因是「初級英語檢定測驗」的複試內容，是口說能力測驗，一般人聽到口試都很害怕，尤其是在回答問題的部分，往往不知如何回答。根據初級口說能力測驗的評分標準，發音語調的正確及流暢度，與文法字彙的正確性，是同等重要，各佔總分的 50%，因此讀者在準備複試時，要把握流暢度和正確性的原則。

　　書中朗讀的部分，是由美籍播音員所錄製而成，語調及發音非常純正，讀者可以多練習幾遍。所有試題也均附有詳細的中文翻譯及單字註解，節省讀者查字典的時間。本書內的問答題，全部經過「劉毅英文初級英檢複試班」，實際在課堂上使用過，效果奇佳。

　　感謝這麼多讀者，不斷地給我們支持與鼓勵。編輯好書，是「學習」一貫的宗旨，我們的目標是，**學英文的書，「學習」都有；「學習」出版，天天進步。**也盼望讀者們不吝給我們批評指正。

編者 謹識

本書製作過程

感謝「劉毅英文初級英檢複試班」的同學們，在上課期間，提供許多寶貴的意見，讓這些試題更加完善。也感謝林銀姿老師，協助編寫詳解及錄音工作，也要感謝美籍老師 Laura E. Stewart 和謝靜芳老師，再三仔細校訂，白雪嬌小姐負責封面設計，黃淑貞小姐負責版面設計，蘇淑玲小姐協助排版。

全民英語能力分級檢定測驗
初級口說能力測驗①

*請在 15 秒內完成並唸出下列自我介紹的句子，請開始：

My seat number is （複試座位號碼）, and my test number is （初試准考證號碼）.

I. 複誦

共五題。題目不印在試題上，經由耳機播出，每題播出兩次，兩次之間約有 1～2 秒的間隔。聽完兩次後，請立即複誦一次。

II. 朗讀句子及短文

共有五個句子及一篇短文，請先利用 1 分鐘的時間閱讀試卷上的句子與短文，然後在 1 分鐘內以正常的速度，清楚正確的朗讀一遍。

One : I live around the corner.
Two : Mary walks to school every day.
Three : Thank you for being so nice to me.
Four : David's office is on top of that building.
Five : The bus will be here in fifteen minutes.

Six　：David works for a construction company.
As he was leaving for work, his wife said,
"Be careful, dear, or you will get hurt.
Working on buildings is dangerous work."
"That's alright, dear," said David. "I
borrowed one hundred dollars from the
boss. So he won't ask me to do dangerous
work."

III. 回答問題

共七題。題目不印在試題上，經由耳機播出，每題播出兩次，兩次之間約有 1~2 秒的間隔。聽完兩次後，請立即回答，每題回答時間 15 秒，請在作答時間內儘量的表達。

* 請將下列自我介紹的句子再唸一遍，請開始：

My seat number is （複試座位號碼）, and my test
number is （初試准考證號碼）.

初級口說能力測驗 ① 詳解

* 請在 15 秒內完成並唸出下列自我介紹的句子，請開始：

My seat number is （複試座位號碼）, and my test number
is （初試准考證號碼）.

I. 複誦

共五題。題目不印在試題上，經由耳機播出，每題播出兩
次，兩次之間約有 1～2 秒的間隔。聽完兩次後，請立即
複誦一次。

1. Let's go! 咱們走吧！

2. What are you doing? 你正在做什麼？

3. How was your lunch?
   你午餐吃得如何？

4. He will come see you in a moment.
   他馬上會來看你。

5. I want to buy that book.
   我想買那本書。

   【註】 *come see you* 來看你（= *come and see you*）
   　　 moment〔'momənt〕*n.* 瞬間；片刻
   　　 in a moment 馬上；立刻

II. 朗讀句子及短文

共有五個句子及一篇短文，請先利用 1 分鐘的時間閱讀試卷上的句子與短文，然後在 1 分鐘內以正常的速度，清楚正確的朗讀一遍。

One ： I live around the corner.
我住在轉角處。

Two ： Mary walks to school every day.
瑪麗每天走路去上學。

Three ： Thank you for being so nice to me.
謝謝你對我這麼好。

Four ： David's office is on top of that building.
大衛的辦公室在那棟大樓的頂樓。

Five ： The bus will be here in fifteen minutes.
巴士再過十五分鐘就會到了。

【註】 corner〔'kɔrnɚ〕n. 轉角
nice〔naɪs〕adj. 好的
office〔'ɔfɪs〕n. 辦公室
top〔tɑp〕n. 頂部
building〔'bɪldɪŋ〕n. 建築物；大樓

Six : David works for a construction company. As he was leaving for work, his wife said, "Be careful, dear, or you will get hurt. Working on buildings is dangerous work." "That's alright, dear," said David. "I borrowed one hundred dollars from the boss. So he won't ask me to do dangerous work."

大衛在一間建築公司上班。當他要去上班的時候,他的太太說:「親愛的,小心一點,不然你會受傷。蓋房子是很危險的工作。」「沒關係,親愛的」大衛說。「我跟老板借了一百塊,所以他不會叫我去做危險的工作。」

【註】 construction〔kən'strʌkʃən〕n. 建築
　　　 company〔'kʌmpənɪ〕n. 公司
　　　 as〔æz〕conj. 當…的時候　　　 *leave for* 動身前往
　　　 work〔wɝk〕n. 工作的地方;工作
　　　 wife〔waɪf〕n. 妻子
　　　 careful〔'kɛrfəl〕adj. 小心的　　　 *get hurt* 受傷
　　　 work on sth. 從事(某種工作)
　　　 dangerous〔'dendʒərəs〕adj. 危險的
　　　 alright〔'ɔl'raɪt〕adj. 沒問題的
　　　 borrow〔'baro〕v. 借(入)
　　　 boss〔bɔs〕n. 老板

Ⅲ. 回答問題

共七題。題目不印在試題上,經由耳機播出,每題播出兩次,兩次之間約有 1～2 秒的間隔。聽完兩次後,請立即回答,每題回答時間 15 秒,請在作答時間內儘量的表達。

1. Q : What is your favorite sport? Why?
  你最喜歡的運動是什麼?為什麼?

A1 : My favorite sport is baseball. I like to play baseball very much because it is an exciting game.
  我最喜歡的運動是棒球。我很喜歡打棒球,因為棒球是很刺激的遊戲。

A2 : My favorite sport is swimming. Swimming is good exercise and it's fun.
  我最喜歡的運動是游泳。游泳是很不錯的運動,並且也很好玩。

【註】 favorite〔'fevərɪt〕adj. 最喜愛的
  sport〔sport〕n. 運動
  baseball〔'bes,bɔl〕n. 棒球
  exciting〔ɪk'saɪtɪŋ〕adj. 刺激的
  swimming〔'swɪmɪŋ〕n. 游泳
  exercise〔'ɛksə,saɪz〕n. 運動
  fun〔fʌn〕adj. 有趣的

2. Q ： What did you eat last night?

你昨天晚上吃了什麼？

A1 ： I ate some street food last night. The food tasted so bad that I threw up right away. I don't know why people still allow that man to sell his disgusting food. I am lucky I am still alive!

我昨天晚上吃了一些路邊攤的東西。那個東西難吃死了，害我一吃下去就吐出來。我不知道爲什麼大家還讓那個人賣那麼噁心的東西。我還活著算我命大。

A2 ： I didn't eat last night because I am too fat and I want to go on a diet. I am afraid if I don't go on a diet, I will turn into a big fat pig.

我昨天晚上沒吃，因爲我太胖了，所以我想要節食。我怕我如果不減肥的話，我會變成一隻大肥豬。

【註】 ***street food*** 路邊攤的食物

taste〔test〕*v.* 嚐起來　　***throw up*** 嘔吐

right away 馬上　　allow〔əˋlaʊ〕*v.* 允許

disgusting〔dɪsˋgʌstɪŋ〕*adj.* 噁心的

lucky〔ˋlʌkɪ〕*adj.* 幸運的

alive〔əˋlaɪv〕*adj.* 活著的　***go on a diet*** 節食

afraid〔əˋfred〕*adj.* 害怕的　　***turn into*** 變成

A3 : My mom cooked dinner last night so I ate
at home. I don't remember what I ate but
the food was good.

我媽媽昨晚有煮晚餐，所以我在家吃。我不記得
我吃了什麼，不過吃得還不錯。

---

3. Q ： How did you get here today?
你今天是怎麼來的？

A1 : My father drove me here today and he will
take me home after I am done here.

我爸爸今天開車載我來的，而且我這邊結束後，
他會來接我回家。

A2 : I took a bus here and it was very crowded.
我搭公車來的，公車很擠。

【註】 remember〔rɪˈmɛmbɚ〕v. 記得
drive sb. 開車載某人
done〔dʌn〕*adj.* 做完的
crowded〔ˈkraʊdɪd〕*adj.* 擁擠的

4. Q ： How is the weather today?

今天的天氣如何？

A1 ： It is sunny and warm today. It's a perfect day to go outside.

今天的天氣風和日麗，是出去玩的好日子。

A2 ： It's raining outside. It has been raining for days. I wonder if it will ever stop raining.

外面正在下雨。已經下了好幾天的雨了。我在想會不會永遠下個不停。

【註】 weather〔'wɛðɚ〕n. 天氣

sunny〔'sʌnɪ〕adj. 晴朗的

warm〔wɔrm〕adj. 溫暖的

perfect〔'pɝfɪkt〕adj. 完美的

outside〔'aʊt'saɪd〕adv. 到外面

wonder〔'wʌndɚ〕v. 想知道

if〔ɪf〕conj. 是否

ever〔'ɛvɚ〕adv. 究竟

stop + V-ing 停止～

5. Q : What is your favorite food? Why?
你最喜歡吃什麼東西？為什麼？

A1 : I love hamburgers. They are tasty and convenient. I especially like the ones from Burger King. Mmmm, just thinking about them makes my mouth water.
我最喜歡吃漢堡了。漢堡又好吃又方便。我特別喜歡吃漢堡王的漢堡。嗯，光想到我就流口水了。

A2 : I like to eat fruit. Taiwan is a fruit lovers' paradise. Taiwanese farmers can grow any kind of fruit, like guavas, pears, peaches, persimmons, pomelos, bell fruits and star fruits. You name it, Taiwan's got it.
我喜歡吃水果。台灣是水果愛好者的天堂。台灣的農夫會種任何種類的水果，像是芭樂、梨子、桃子、柿子、柚子、蓮霧和楊桃。你想到的，台灣都有。

【註】 hamburger〔'hæmbɝgɚ〕n. 漢堡

tasty〔'testɪ〕adj. 可口的

convenient〔kən'vinjənt〕adj. 方便的

especially〔ə'spɛʃəlɪ〕adv. 尤其

think about 想到　　mouth〔mauθ〕n. 嘴巴

water〔'wɔtɚ〕v. 流口水

fruit〔frut〕n. 水果　　lover〔'lʌvɚ〕n. 愛好者

paradise〔'pærə,daɪs〕n. 天堂

Taiwanese〔,taɪwə'niz〕adj. 台灣的

farmer〔'fɑrmɚ〕n. 農夫

grow〔gro〕v. 種植　　kind〔kaɪnd〕n. 種類

like〔laɪk〕prep. 像是

guava〔'gwɑvə〕n. 芭樂　　pear〔pɛr〕n. 梨子

peach〔pitʃ〕n. 桃子

persimmon〔pɚ'sɪmən〕n. 柿子

pomelo〔'pɑməlo〕n. 柚子

bell fruit 蓮霧（= *wax apple*）

　　【台灣獨有產品，一般字典查不到。】

star fruit 楊桃

name〔nem〕v. 說出…的名字

you name it 你要什麼儘管說

have got 有

6. Q ： What is your favorite TV show? Why?

你最喜歡的電視節目是什麼？爲什麼？

A1 ： My favorite TV show is *The Garden of The Shooting Stars*. I like to watch that show because it is very romantic. All the people in the show are so cool and I wish I could be like them.

我最喜歡的電視節目是「流星花園」。我喜歡看那個節目，因爲它的劇情很浪漫。戲裡面的人都很酷，我希望能像他們一樣。

A2 ： I don't really like to watch TV that much, so I don't have a favorite TV show. I like to play PC games better, especially *Half-life*. It is very exciting and I can kill a lot of bad people, too.

我不大喜歡看電視，所以我沒有最喜歡的電視節目。我比較喜歡玩電腦遊戲，尤其是「戰慄時空」。那個遊戲很刺激，而且我還可以殺很多壞人。

【註】 *TV show* 電視節目　　garden〔ˋgɑrdn〕*n.* 花園
shooting star 流星
romantic〔roˋmæntɪk〕*adj.* 浪漫的
cool〔kul〕*adj.* 酷的　　*PC games* 電玩遊戲
Half-life 戰慄時空（電腦遊戲軟體的名稱）

7. Q ： What are you going to do later?
　　　你待會兒會做什麼？

A1 ： Well, I don't plan on staying here all
　　　morning, so I'm just gonna go home. Boy!
　　　That was a stupid question!
　　　嗯，我並不打算一整個早上都待在這裡，所以
　　　我會回家。真是的！怎麼會問那麼笨的問題呢！

A2 ： I think mý parents will take me out to
　　　celebrate the conclusion of this test. After
　　　that, I'm gonna pray to God that I will pass
　　　the test.
　　　我爸媽大概會帶我出去，慶祝考試考完了。然後
　　　我會向上帝禱告，希望我能通過這個測驗。

【註】　later〔'letɚ〕adv. 待會兒
　　　gonna〔'ɡɑnə〕【口語】將要（= going to）
　　　plan on + *V-ing* 計劃～；打算～（= *plan* + *to V.*）
　　　boy〔bɔɪ〕interj. 真是的
　　　stupid〔'stjupɪd〕adj. 愚蠢的
　　　celebrate〔'sɛlə,bret〕v. 慶祝
　　　conclusion〔kən'kluʒən〕n. 結束
　　　pray〔pre〕v. 祈禱　　God〔ɡɑd〕n. 上帝
　　　pass〔pæs〕v. 通過；（考試）及格

A3 : I don't know what I will do later. If I could predict the future, then I wouldn't have to take this test. I'd just go buy lottery tickets and be rich.

我不知道我等一下會做些什麼事。我要是能未卜先知的話,我就不用考這個試了。我就會去買樂透,然後變成大富翁。

【註】 predict〔prɪˋdɪkt〕v. 預測
　　　future〔ˋfjutʃə〕n. 未來
　　　test〔tɛst〕n. 考試　**take a test** 參加考試
　　　go buy 去買 (= *go and buy*)
　　　lottery〔ˋlɑtərɪ〕n. 樂透
　　　ticket〔ˋtɪkɪt〕n. 票;券
　　　rich〔rɪtʃ〕adj. 有錢的

* 請將下列自我介紹的句子再唸一遍,請開始:

My seat number is (複試座位號碼) , and my test number is (初試准考證號碼).

全民英語能力分級檢定測驗

初級口說能力測驗②

*請在15秒內完成並唸出下列自我介紹的句子,請開始:

My seat number is （複試座位號碼）, and my test
number is （初試准考證號碼）.

I. 複誦

共五題。題目不印在試題上,經由耳機播出,每題播出兩
次,兩次之間約有 1~2 秒的間隔。聽完兩次後,請立即
複誦一次。

II. 朗讀句子及短文

共有五個句子及一篇短文,請先利用 1 分鐘的時間閱讀試
卷上的句子與短文,然後在 1 分鐘內以正常的速度,清楚
正確的朗讀一遍。

One   : How about you and I going bicycling this
        Sunday?
Two   : Would you pass me the pepper, please?
Three : Hurry up, or you will be late!

Four : Would you like to come to my home for dinner tonight?

Five : That island is known for its beautiful scenery.

Six : Tom's parrot can talk. It's very smart. Every morning at seven it says "Wake up!" in a very loud voice. Tom doesn't need to use his alarm clock because his bird wakes him up.

Ⅲ. 回答問題

共七題。題目不印在試題上，經由耳機播出，每題播出兩次，兩次之間約有 1～2 秒的間隔。聽完兩次後，請立即回答，每題回答時間 15 秒，請在作答時間內儘量的表達。

* 請將下列自我介紹的句子再唸一遍，請開始：

My seat number is （複試座位號碼）, and my test number is （初試准考證號碼）.

初級口說能力測驗②詳解

* 請在 15 秒內完成並唸出下列自我介紹的句子，請開始：

My seat number is （複試座位號碼）, and my test number is （初試准考證號碼）.

I. 複誦

共五題。題目不印在試題上，經由耳機播出，每題播出兩次，兩次之間約有 1～2 秒的間隔。聽完兩次後，請立即複誦一次。

1. Don't go into that house!
   不要進去那間房子！

2. Wait for me! 等我！

3. Did you have a great time?
   你玩得愉快嗎？

4. He is satisfied with his car.
   他很滿意自己的車。

5. It is so kind of you to say so.
   你這麼說，人真好。

【註】 *wait for* 等待　　*have a great time* 玩得愉快
satisfied〔'sætɪs,faɪd〕*adj.* 滿意的 < *with* >
kind〔kaɪnd〕*adj.* 好心的

II. 朗讀句子及短文

共有五個句子及一篇短文，請先利用 1 分鐘的時間閱讀試卷上的句子與短文，然後在 1 分鐘內以正常的速度，清楚正確的朗讀一遍。

One ： How about you and I going bicycling this Sunday? 我們這個星期天去騎腳踏車怎麼樣？

Two ： Would you pass me the pepper, please? 可不可以請你把胡椒遞給我？

Three ： Hurry up, or you will be late! 快一點，不然你會遲到！

Four ： Would you like to come to my home for dinner tonight? 你今晚來我家吃晚飯好不好？

Five ： That island is known for its beautiful scenery. 那座島以美麗的風景而有名。

【註】 *How about + V-ing?* 做～如何？（表提議）
bicycle〔'baɪsɪkḷ〕v. 騎腳踏車
pass〔pæs〕v. 傳遞
pepper〔'pɛpɚ〕n. 胡椒粉　　*hurry up* 趕快
or〔ɔr〕conj. 否則　　*would like to V.* 想要
island〔'aɪlənd〕n. 島
be known for ～ 以～而有名
scenery〔'sinərɪ〕n. 風景

Six : Tom's parrot can talk. It's very smart. Every morning at seven it says "Wake up!" in a very loud voice. Tom doesn't need to use his alarm clock because his bird wakes him up.

湯姆的鸚鵡會講話。牠很聰明。每天早上七點的時候，牠會很大聲地叫：「起床了！」所以湯姆不需要用到鬧鐘，因為他的鳥會叫他起床。

Ⅲ. 回答問題

共七題。題目不印在試題上，經由耳機播出，每題播出兩次，兩次之間約有 1～2 秒的間隔。聽完兩次後，請立即回答，每題回答時間 15 秒，請在作答時間內儘量的表達。

1. Q ： What time did you go to bed last night? Why?

你昨天晚上幾點上床睡覺？為什麼？

【註】 parrot〔'pærət〕n. 鸚鵡

smart〔smɑrt〕adj. 聰明的

wake up 起床

loud〔laʊd〕adj. 大聲的

voice〔vɔɪs〕n. 聲音

alarm clock 鬧鐘

wake sb. up 叫某人起床

A1 : I went to bed early last night. Maybe around nine o'clock or so. I was too tired to remember what time it was.

我昨晚很早就睡了。大概九點多吧。我累得忘掉到底是幾點了。

A2 : I went to bed at about midnight last night. I stayed up to watch my favorite TV show. I had such a good time that I didn't feel tired.

我昨晚大概十二點左右去睡覺。我熬夜是為了要看我最喜歡的電視節目。我看得很高興,所以一點都不覺得累。

【註】 maybe〔'mebɪ〕 *adv.* 大概;或許
　　　 around〔ə'raʊnd〕 *prep.* 大約;將近
　　　 or so 大約　　*too…to~* 太…以致於不~
　　　 midnight〔'mɪd͵naɪt〕 *n.* 半夜十二點
　　　 stay up 熬夜　favorite〔'fevərɪt〕 *adj.* 最喜愛的
　　　 TV show 電視節目
　　　 have a good time 玩得很愉快;看得很高興
　　　 such…that~ 如此的…以致於~

A3 : I didn't sleep last night because I played
PC games until this morning, and then I
came here to take this test.

我昨晚沒睡，因為我玩電玩遊戲玩到今天早上，
然後我就來這裡參加考試了。

～～～～～～～～～～～～～～～～

2. Q : Please give a brief description of your family.

請簡單描述你的家庭。

A1 : There are four people in my family. My
parents are both teachers and my older
brother is in college now. We also have a
cat named Kitty.

我的家裡有四個人。我的父母都是老師，我的哥哥
現在在讀大學。我們還有一隻貓，名字叫做凱蒂。

【註】 *PC games* 電玩遊戲
　　　 until〔ən'tɪl〕*prep.* 直到
　　　 then〔ðɛn〕*adv.* 然後　　　 test〔tɛst〕*n.* 考試
　　　 take a test 參加考試
　　　 brief〔brif〕*adj.* 簡短的
　　　 description〔dɪ'skrɪpʃən〕*n.* 描述
　　　 older brother 哥哥
　　　 college〔'kɑlɪdʒ〕*n.* 大學　　　 *named* ~ 名叫 ~

A2 : I have a big family. There are my parents and grandparents, I also have two brothers and three sisters. We all live in one great big house. We don't have any pets, but I would like to have one, maybe a dog or something.

我們家是個大家族。家裡有父母和祖父母，我還有兩個哥哥和三個姊姊。我們全部住在一間大房子裡。我們沒有養寵物，但是我想要養一隻。也許一隻狗之類的吧。

A3 : There are only three people in my family. I am the only child. We have two dogs named Dog and Cat.

我們家裡只有三個人。我是獨生子（女）。我們有兩隻狗，一隻叫狗，另外一隻叫貓。

---

3. Q ： What kind of music do you like most? Why do you like it?

你最喜歡什麼樣的音樂？你為什麼會喜歡它？

【註】 grandparents〔'grænd,pɛrənts〕*n. pl.* 祖父母
pet〔pɛt〕*n.* 寵物　　*or something* 或什麼的
only child 獨生子；獨生女

A1： I like to listen to hip-hop a lot because I can dance to the tunes.

我很喜歡聽嘻哈音樂，因為我可以隨歌起舞。

A2： I don't like to listen to music at all. I don't know why I don't like it; maybe I have a dull and boring life.

我一點都不喜歡聽音樂。我也不知道為什麼我不喜歡；也許我過著乏味無聊的生活。

4. Q ： What kind of fruit do you like most? Why?

你最喜歡的水果是哪一種？為什麼？

A1： I love to eat watermelon. Watermelon is sweet and juicy. Nothing can satisfy my thirst better than watermelon.

我最喜歡吃西瓜了。西瓜又甜又多汁。西瓜最能滿足我的渴望。

【註】 **hip-hop** 嘻哈音樂　　tune〔tjun〕*n.* 曲調
　　　not…at all 一點也不…　　dull〔dʌl〕*adj.* 乏味的
　　　boring〔'borɪŋ〕*adj.* 無聊的
　　　watermelon〔'wɔtə‚mɛlən〕*n.* 西瓜
　　　juicy〔'dʒusɪ〕*adj.* 多汁的
　　　satisfy〔'sætɪs‚faɪ〕*v.* 使滿足
　　　thirst〔θɜst〕*n.* 口渴；渴望

A2 : Strawberries are my favorite fruit. The fragrance of a strawberry is wonderful. The sweet and tangy taste is so addictive and unforgettable that I can't stop eating them.

草莓是我最喜歡吃的水果。草莓的香味眞美妙。那香甜濃烈的味道，眞是令人著迷又難忘，讓我無法不去品嚐它。

5. Q : If you were taking a bath and an earthquake struck, what would you do?

如果你正在洗澡的時候，突然有地震來襲，你會怎麼辦？

【註】 strawberry〔'strɔ,bɛrɪ〕n. 草莓
fragrance〔'fregrəns〕n. 香味
wonderful〔'wʌndəfəl〕adj. 很棒的
tangy〔'tæŋɪ〕adj. 有濃烈香味的
taste〔test〕n. 滋味
addictive〔ə'dɪktɪv〕adj. 使人上癮的
unforgettable〔,ʌnfə'gɛtəbḷ〕adj. 令人難忘的
take a bath 洗澡
earthquake〔'ɝθ,kwek〕n. 地震
strike〔straɪk〕v. 來襲（三態變化爲：strike-struck -struck）

A1 : I would scream and run out of the house.
But before I did that, I would remember
to get dressed first.
我會大叫，然後跑到屋子外面。但是在我那樣做
之前，我會記得先把衣服穿好。

A2 : I would first put on my clothes, then I would
turn off the gas and run out into the open as
fast as I could.
我會先把衣服穿好，然後我會把瓦斯關掉，再
儘快跑到空地去。

A3 : I would not do anything. I am so used to
earthquakes in Taiwan that I am immune to
them. Nothing is ever going to happen
anyway.
我什麼都不會做。我已經太習慣台灣的地震了，
我已經免疫了。反正也不會發生什麼事。

【註】 scream 〔 skrim 〕 v. 尖叫
get dressed 穿好衣服   *put on* 穿上衣服
turn off 關掉   gas 〔 gæs 〕 n. 瓦斯
open 〔'opən 〕 n. 戶外；空地
as…as one can 儘可能   *be used to* 習慣於
immune 〔 ɪ'mjun 〕 adj. 免疫的
ever 〔'ɛvə 〕 adv. 曾經
anyway 〔'ɛnɪ,we 〕 adv. 反正

6. Q : What is your favorite drink? Why?

你最喜歡的飲料是什麼？爲什麼？

A1 : My favorite drink is Qoo juice. I like it because the packaging is very colorful and attractive. It is also a popular drink among my friends. I guess if you don't drink Qoo, you are not cool.

我最喜歡喝酷果汁。我喜歡喝酷果汁，是因爲它的包裝很亮麗又吸引人。它在我的朋友之間也很流行。我認爲不喝酷果汁的話，你就不夠酷。

A2 : I love pearl milk tea. The pearls are chewy and the milk tea is sweet and creamy. I wouldn't drink anything else.

我最喜歡珍珠奶茶了。珍珠有嚼勁，奶茶香甜可口。我只喝珍珠奶茶。

【註】 packaging〔'pækɪdʒɪŋ〕n. 包裝
colorful〔'kʌləfəl〕adj. 色彩鮮豔的
attractive〔ə'træktɪv〕adj. 吸引人的
popular〔'pɑpjələ〕adj. 受歡迎的
guess〔gɛs〕v. 認爲　　cool〔kul〕adj. 酷的
pearl〔pɝl〕n. 珍珠　　*milk tea* 奶茶
pearl milk tea 珍珠奶茶
chewy〔'tʃuɪ〕adj. 有嚼勁的
creamy〔'krimɪ〕adj. 多乳脂的

7. Q : Do you like to take the bus?　Why or why not?

　　　你喜不喜歡搭公車？爲什麼或爲什麼不？

　A1 : I don't know about buses because I don't
　　　take buses.　My parents will take me
　　　wherever I want to go.　Besides, I can ride
　　　my bicycle when my parents are busy.

　　　我不太懂公車，因爲我不搭公車。我爸媽會帶我
　　　去任何我想要去的地方。此外，我爸媽忙的時候，
　　　我可以騎腳踏車。

　A2 : I think Taipei City has the best bus service
　　　in Taiwan.　The buses go anywhere you
　　　want to go.　I don't know what I would do
　　　without the buses.

　　　我認爲台北的公車是全台灣最棒的。公車會帶你
　　　去任何你想去的地方。要是沒公車的話，我不知
　　　道該如何是好。

【註】　wherever〔hwɛr'ɛvɚ〕*conj.*　無論何處
　　　besides〔bɪ'saɪdz〕*adv.*　此外
　　　ride〔raɪd〕*v.*　騎
　　　service〔'sɝvɪs〕*n.*　公共設施

A3： I hate taking the bus! The buses are often
crowded. There are never any open seats.
We are all forced to squeeze in there like
sardines, and the people on the buses smell
bad, too.

我最討厭坐公車了！公車上經常人很多，而且都
會沒有位子。我們都要像沙丁魚一樣地擠進公車
裡，還有車上的人都很臭。

【註】 crowded〔'kraudɪd〕adj. 擁擠的

open〔'opən〕adj. 空著的

force〔fors〕v. 強迫

squeeze〔skwiz〕v. 擠

sardine〔sɑr'din〕n. 沙丁魚

smell〔smɛl〕v. 聞起來

*請將下列自我介紹的句子再唸一遍，請開始：

My seat number is （複試座位號碼）, and my test number
is （初試准考證號碼）.

全民英語能力分級檢定測驗
初級口說能力測驗③

*請在15秒內完成並唸出下列自我介紹的句子，請開始：

My seat number is （複試座位號碼）, and my test
number is （初試准考證號碼）.

Ⅰ. 複誦

共五題。題目不印在試題上，經由耳機播出，每題播出兩
次，兩次之間約有 1～2 秒的間隔。聽完兩次後，請立即
複誦一次。

Ⅱ. 朗讀句子及短文

共有五個句子及一篇短文，請先利用 1 分鐘的時間閱讀試
卷上的句子與短文，然後在 1 分鐘內以正常的速度，清楚
正確的朗讀一遍。

One　： Jimmy stayed out all day long.

Two　： The meal was wonderful, wasn't it?

Three： My father likes to listen to classical music.

Four　： You need to go get a haircut today.

Five : I didn't go to school today because I was
sick.

Six : Bob and Nancy went out for dinner at a
famous restaurant last night. They had to
wait an hour before they could get a table.
They waited another thirty minutes before
they got their food.

III. 回答問題

共七題。題目不印在試題上，經由耳機播出，每題播出兩
次，兩次之間約有 1～2 秒的間隔。聽完兩次後，請立即
回答，每題回答時間 15 秒，請在作答時間內儘量的表達。

*請將下列自我介紹的句子再唸一遍，請開始：

My seat number is (複試座位號碼) , and my test
number is (初試准考證號碼) .

初級口說能力測驗③詳解

＊請在 15 秒內完成並唸出下列自我介紹的句子，請開始：

My seat number is （複試座位號碼）, and my test number is （初試准考證號碼）.

I. 複誦

共五題。題目不印在試題上，經由耳機播出，每題播出兩次，兩次之間約有 1～2 秒的間隔。聽完兩次後，請立即複誦一次。

1. I don't remember that book. 我不記得那本書。

2. Did anyone call today? 今天有人打過電話來嗎？

3. She helped her mother cook. 她幫她媽媽煮飯。

4. The book is hard to understand. 這本書很難懂。

5. The weather is nice today. 天氣今天很好。

　　【註】 remember〔rɪˋmɛmbɚ〕v. 記得
　　　　　 understand〔͵ʌndɚˋstænd〕v. 了解

II. 朗讀句子及短文

共有五個句子及一篇短文，請先利用 1 分鐘的時間閱讀試卷上的句子與短文，然後在 1 分鐘內以正常的速度，清楚正確的朗讀一遍。

One ： Jimmy stayed out all day long.
吉米一整天都得在外面。

Two ： The meal was wonderful, wasn't it?
那一餐眞棒，對不對？

Three： My father likes to listen to classical music.
我爸爸喜歡聽古典音樂。

Four ： You need to go get a haircut today.
你今天必須要去剪頭髮了。

Five ： I didn't go to school today because I was sick.
我今天因爲生病而沒去上學。

Six ： Bob and Nancy went out for dinner at a famous
restaurant last night. They had to wait an hour
before they could get a table. They waited
another thirty minutes before they got their food.
鮑伯和南西昨天晚上去一間有名的餐廳吃晚餐。他們
等了一個鐘頭才有位子坐。他們又等了三十分鐘才吃
到東西。

【註】 *stay out* 待在戶外；不在家
all day long 一整天
classical〔'klæsɪkḷ〕*adj.* 古典的
haircut〔'hɛrˌkʌt〕*n.* 理髮
famous〔'feməs〕*adj.* 有名的

III. 回答問題

共七題。題目不印在試題上，經由耳機播出，每題播出兩次，兩次之間約有 1～2 秒的間隔。聽完兩次後，請立即回答，每題回答時間 15 秒，請在作答時間內儘量的表達。

1. Q : Do you like to eat at home? Why or why not?
　　　你喜歡在家吃嗎？為什麼或為什麼不？

　　A1 : I love eating at home. My mother is a great cook. She can cook all my favorite food.
　　　我喜歡在家裡吃。我媽媽很會做菜。她會煮我最喜歡吃的東西。

　　A2 : I don't eat at home very often because I always have to go to cram schools after school.
　　　我不常在家裡吃，因為我放學後往往要去補習班。

　　A3 : I don't like to eat at home. Restaurants offer more choices.
　　　我不喜歡在家吃。餐廳提供比較多的選擇。

【註】favorite (ˈfevərɪt) adj. 最喜愛的
　　　　cram school 補習班　　*after school* 放學後
　　　　offer (ˈɔfə) v. 提供　　choice (tʃɔɪs) n. 選擇

2. Q : What do you do when you get sick?
你生病的時候怎麼辦？

A1 : I go see a doctor right away.
我馬上去看醫生。

A2 : I stay home and have my mother take care
of me. 我待在家裡，讓我媽媽照顧我。

A3 : I don't do anything because I am a healthy
boy and I will feel better soon.
我什麼都不做，因為我很健康，所以我很快就會
好了。

~~~~~~~~~~~~~~~~~~~~~~~~~~~~~~~~~

3. Q : What time did you get up this morning?
你今天早上幾點起床？

A1 : I got up at eight o'clock this morning. I
would have slept in but I had to come here
to take this test.
我今天早上八點起床。我本來可以睡晚一點，但
是我要來這裡考試。

【註】 *right away* 立刻　　*take care of* 照顧
healthy〔ˈhɛlθɪ〕*adj.* 健康的
would have + *p.p.* 本來可以～
sleep in 晚起床

A2： I woke up at about four o'clock. I was too nervous to sleep well.

我大約四點鐘醒過來。我太緊張了,所以沒睡好。

A3： I always wake up at 5:30 in the morning, and today was no different.

我都會在早上五點半起床,今天也一樣。

4. Q ： How many CDs do you have?

你有幾片 CD ?

A1： I don't have any music CDs but I have a lot on language learning. I listen to them every day so my language ability will improve.

我沒有音樂的 CD,但是我有很多學語言的 CD。
我每天都聽,這樣我的語言能力才會進步。

【註】 *wake up* 醒過來;起床
too…to V. 太…以致於不~
nervous〔'nɜvəs〕*adj.* 緊張的
different〔'dɪfrənt〕*adj.* 不同的
on〔ɑn〕*prep.* 有關
language〔'læŋgwɪdʒ〕*n.* 語言
ability〔ə'bɪlətɪ〕*n.* 能力
improve〔ɪm'pruv〕*v.* 改善;進步

A2 : I don't have any because I don't listen to music.

我一片都沒有，因為我不聽音樂。

A3 : I have maybe twenty CDs or so. They are all my favorite music. I like them very much.

我大概有二十幾片 CD。全部都是我最喜歡的音樂。我很喜歡它們。

5. Q : What is your favorite subject in school? Why?

你在學校最喜歡的科目是什麼？為什麼？

A1 : My favorite subject is English. It is important for everyone to have good English ability. That is why I like English so much.

我最喜歡的科目是英文。有良好的英文能力，對每個人而言都是很重要的。這就是我為什麼那麼喜歡英文。

【註】 *or so* 大約　　favorite〔ˋfevərɪt〕 *adj.* 最喜愛的
　　　　 n. 最喜愛的人或物
　　　　subject〔ˋsʌbdʒɪkt〕 *n.* 科目
　　　　important〔ɪmˋpɔrtn̩t〕 *adj.* 重要的

A2 : I like all the subjects so I don't have a
favorite. I want to be a jack-of-all-trades.
所有的科目我都喜歡，所以我沒有最喜歡的科
目。我要當一個什麼都會的人。

A3 : My favorite is history. It is always interesting
to read about what happened in the past and
we can also learn from it.
我最喜歡歷史。讀到以前發生過什麼事，總是很
有趣，而且我們還可以從中學習。

6. Q : What is your favorite movie? Why?
你最喜歡的電影是什麼？為什麼？

A1 : My favorite movie is *Godzilla*. The special
effects in that movie are so great. It was
also pretty scary.
我最喜歡的電影是「酷斯拉」。那部電影的特效
超棒的，而且也蠻恐怖的。

【註】　trade〔tred〕*n.* 手藝；職業
　　　　jack-of-all-trades 能做多種不同工作的人；
　　　　　什麼都會的人　　*in the past* 過去
　　　　special effect 特效　　pretty〔'prɪtɪ〕*adv.* 相當
　　　　scary〔'skɛrɪ〕*adj.* 恐怖的

A2 : My favorite movie is *American Pie*. This
movie showed us what American teenagers
are like and it was very funny.
我最喜歡看「美國派」。這部電影告訴我們美國
青少年是什麼樣子，而且也很好笑。

7. Q ： What do you like to do on weekends?
你週末喜歡做些什麼？

A1 : I like to stay home and do nothing, but I
can never do that because I have to go to
cram school all the time.
我喜歡待在家裡，什麼都不做，但是我無法這麼
做，因為我都得去補習。

A2 : I like to go out and play basketball with my
friends. 我喜歡和我的朋友出去打籃球。

【註】 show〔ʃo〕v. 顯示
teenager〔'tin‚edʒɚ〕n. 青少年
all the time 總是

A3： I like to go to the Taipei City Youth Activity
　　　Center on weekends. I can do a lot of things
　　　there. I can go on the Internet or read comic
　　　books. There are also many activities I can
　　　participate in. It is the most wonderful place
　　　on earth.

我週末時喜歡去台北市青少年活動中心。我可以
在那裡做很多事。我可以上網或看漫畫。那裡還
有許多活動能讓我參加。那裡真是全天下最好的
地方。

【註】 weekend〔'wik'ɛnd〕n. 週末
　　　 activity〔æk'tɪvətɪ〕n. 活動
　　　 center〔'sɛntɚ〕n. 中心
　　　 Internet〔'ɪntɚˌnɛt〕n. 網際網路
　　　 comic books 漫畫書
　　　 participate〔par'tɪsəˌpet〕v. 參加 <*in*>
　　　 wonderful〔'wʌndɚfəl〕adj. 很棒的
　　　 earth〔ɝθ〕n. 地球；人間
　　　 on earth 在這地球上；在全世界 (= *in the world*)

*請將下列自我介紹的句子再唸一遍，請開始：

My seat number is （複試座位號碼）, and my test number
is （初試准考證號碼）.

心得筆記欄..........✎

全民英語能力分級檢定測驗

初級口說能力測驗④

* 請在 15 秒內完成並唸出下列自我介紹的句子，請開始：

My seat number is （複試座位號碼）, and my test
number is （初試准考證號碼）.

I. 複誦

共五題。題目不印在試題上，經由耳機播出，每題播出兩
次，兩次之間約有 1～2 秒的間隔。聽完兩次後，請立即
複誦一次。

II. 朗讀句子及短文

共有五個句子及一篇短文，請先利用 1 分鐘的時間閱讀試
卷上的句子與短文，然後在 1 分鐘內以正常的速度，清楚
正確的朗讀一遍。

One　 : I am afraid you have to go alone.

Two　 : I don't know who that man is.

Three: Who took out the garbage this morning?

Four　: Oranges are rich in vitamin C.

Five　: Please make yourself at home.

Six　：Nowadays computers are used in many places—in shops, offices, schools, and at home.　They are making our lives richer and more comfortable than before.　It is almost impossible to live without computers.

Ⅲ. 回答問題

共七題。題目不印在試題上，經由耳機播出，每題播出兩次，兩次之間約有 1～2 秒的間隔。聽完兩次後，請立即回答，每題回答時間 15 秒，請在作答時間內儘量的表達。

＊請將下列自我介紹的句子再唸一遍，請開始：

My seat number is （複試座位號碼）, and my test number is （初試准考證號碼）.

初級口說能力測驗④詳解

＊請在15秒內完成並唸出下列自我介紹的句子，請開始：

My seat number is （複試座位號碼）, and my test number is （初試准考證號碼）.

I. 複誦

共五題。題目不印在試題上，經由耳機播出，每題播出兩次，兩次之間約有1～2秒的間隔。聽完兩次後，請立即複誦一次。

1. Robert can't go tonight.　羅伯特今晚沒辦法去。

2. I don't know his number.　我不知道他的號碼。

3. I am happy you're going.　我很高興你要去。

4. I want to help you.　我想幫你。

5. Did you hear about the fire?　你知道火災的消息嗎？

【註】 *hear about* 得知　　fire〔faɪr〕*n.* 火災

II. 朗讀句子及短文

共有五個句子及一篇短文，請先利用1分鐘的時間閱讀試卷上的句子與短文，然後在1分鐘內以正常的速度，清楚正確的朗讀一遍。

One : I am afraid you have to go alone.
你恐怕要自己去了。

Two : I don't know who that man is.
我不知道那個人是誰。

Three : Who took out the garbage this morning?
今天早上是誰把垃圾拿出去的？

Four : Oranges are rich in vitamin C.
柳橙有豐富的維他命 C。

Five : Please make yourself at home. 請不要客氣。

Six : Nowadays computers are used in many places—
in shops, offices, schools, and at home. They are
making our lives richer and more comfortable
than before. It is almost impossible to live
without computers.
現今，電腦運用在許多地方——商店、辦公室、學校，
還有在家裡。它們使我們的生活比以前更充實、更舒
適。現在要是沒了電腦，日子就幾乎沒辦法過了。

【註】 rich〔rɪtʃ〕adj. 豐富的 < in >
vitamin〔'vaɪtəmɪn〕n. 維他命
make oneself **at home** 不要客氣；不要拘束
nowadays〔'naʊə,dez〕adv. 現今
impossible〔ɪm'pasəbl̩〕adj. 不可能的

Ⅲ. 回答問題

共七題。題目不印在試題上，經由耳機播出，每題播出兩次，兩次之間約有 1～2 秒的間隔。聽完兩次後，請立即回答，每題回答時間 15 秒，請在作答時間內儘量的表達。

1. Q ： How often do you exercise?

你多久運動一次？

A1 : I don't exercise at all because I don't have time.

我不運動的，因為我沒時間。

A2 : I exercise every day at school during PE class.

我每天在學校上體育課的時候會做運動。

A3 : I will only exercise when I think of it. So I don't really exercise on a regular basis.

我想到才會去做運動。所以我其實不會定時做運動。

【註】 exercise (ˈɛksəˌsaɪz) v. n. 運動

not…at all 一點也不…

during (ˈdjʊrɪŋ) prep. 在…期間

PE 體育 (= *physical education*)

think of 想到　　basis (ˈbesɪs) n. 基準

on a regular basis 定時地

2. Q ： Do you have a cellular phone?　Why or why
    not?　你有沒有行動電話？為什麼或為什麼不？

A1： I don't have a cell phone and I don't think
    I really need one.
    我沒有行動電話，而且我也不認為我有需要。

A2： I have a cell phone.　That way my mom can
    find me whenever she wants.
    我有一隻手機。那樣子我媽媽才可以隨時找到我。

A3： Of course I have a cell phone.　A cell phone
    is very important to have.　I wouldn't know
    what to do without a cell phone.
    我當然有手機囉。手機是很重要的必備品。要是
    沒有手機，我會不知所措。

【註】 cellular〔'sɛljələ〕adj. 蜂窩狀的
    cellular phone 行動電話；手機（= *cell phone*）
    that way 那樣一來
    whenever〔hwɛn'ɛvə〕conj. 每當
    of course 當然
    important〔ɪm'pɔrtn̩t〕adj. 重要的

3. Q ： What did you have for breakfast this morning?　你今天早上吃了什麼早餐？

A1： I had long fritters, baked rolls, and soybean milk.　After eating all those, I topped them off with a bowl of rice soup.

我吃了油條、燒餅，和豆漿。吃完那些之後，我又吃了一碗稀飯。

A2： I had a large American style breakfast with eggs, bacon, hash browns, and toast.

我吃了一大份美式早餐；裡面有蛋、培根、薯餅、和吐司。

【註】 fritter〔ˈfrɪtɚ〕 *adj.* 帶餡油炸麵糰

long fritter 油條　　baked〔bekt〕*adj.* 烤過的

roll〔rol〕*n.* 捲餅　　*baked roll* 燒餅

soybean〔ˈsɔɪˌbin〕*n.* 大豆

soybean milk 豆漿 (= *soy milk* = *bean milk*)

top off 結束　　bowl〔bol〕*n.* 碗

rice soup 稀飯 (= porridge〔ˈpɔrɪdʒ〕

= congee〔ˈkɑndʒi〕)

style〔staɪl〕*n.* 樣式；風格

bacon〔ˈbekən〕*n.* 培根　　*hash browns* 薯餅

toast〔tost〕*n.* 吐司

A3 : I don't eat breakfast because I think breakfast
is a waste of time.
我沒吃早餐，因為我認爲吃早餐很浪費時間。

━━━━━━━━━━━━━━━━━━

4. Q : Do you do household chores? Why or why
not? 你會不會幫忙做家事？爲什麼或爲什麼不？

A1 : Sometimes I help my parents with the dishes
and garbage. But since I am busy all the
time with my schoolwork, I don't do chores
very often.
我有時會幫我父母洗碗和倒垃圾。但是因爲我的
課業太繁忙了，我不常做家事。

A2 : I don't have to do anything because we
have a maid at home and she takes care of
everything.
我什麼都不用做，因爲我們家有女傭，她會做
好所有的家事。

【註】 waste〔west〕n. 浪費
household〔'haʊs,hold〕adj. 家庭的
household chores 家事（= chores〔tʃorz〕）
dishes〔dɪʃ〕n. pl. 碗盤　since〔sɪns〕conj. 因爲
all the time 一直　maid〔med〕n. 女傭
take care of 處理

A3 : I have to do all kinds of household chores, such as washing dishes, taking out the garbage, and mowing the lawn. I do them because I want to help.

我所有的家事都要做，像是洗碗、倒垃圾，和割草。我是因為想幫忙才做的。

~~~~~~

5. Q : How do you go to school every day?
你每天如何去上學？

A1 : I walk to school every day because the school is only a block away from home,
我每天走路去上學，因為學校離家裡只隔一條街。

A2 : My father drives me to school every day on his way to work.
我爸爸每天上班的時候，會順道開車載我去學校。

A3 : I take the MRT to school every day.
我每天搭捷運去上學。

【註】 *such as* 像是 　　mow〔mo〕*v.* 割
lawn〔lɔn〕*n.* 草坪　　block〔blɑk〕*n.* 街區
drive sb. 開車送某人
on one's way to ~ 在某人前往～的途中
MRT 捷運（= *Mass Rapid Transit*）

6. Q : What is your favorite cartoon character?
你最喜歡的卡通人物是誰？

A1 : My favorite cartoon character is Cherry Little Ball. I think she is the cutest cartoon character ever.
我最喜歡的卡通人物是櫻桃小丸子。我覺得她是有史以來最可愛的卡通人物。

【説明】櫻桃小丸子的正式説法是 Maruko。

A2 : I love Little Ding Dong the most. He can do anything. I wish I could have one.
我最愛小叮噹了。他什麼都做得到。我真希望我能有一個小叮噹。

【説明】小叮噹的正式説法是 Doraemon。

━━━━━━━━━━━━━━━━

【註】 favorite〔ˈfevərɪt〕adj. 最喜愛的
cartoon〔kɑrˈtun〕n. 卡通
character〔ˈkærɪktə〕n.（戲劇等的）人物；角色
cherry〔ˈtʃɛrɪ〕n. 櫻桃
cute〔kjut〕adj. 可愛的
ever〔ˈɛvə〕adv. 從來；至今

7. Q ： Your mother wants to cook a big meal for you.
 What would you like your mother to cook?
 你媽媽要做大餐給你吃。你想要她做些什麼？

A1 ： My favorite dish is fried chicken and my
 mother will cook it for me.
 我最喜歡的菜是炸雞，我媽媽會煮給我吃的。

A2 ： I love it when my mother cooks Buddha
 Jumps Over The Wall.
 我最喜歡我媽媽煮佛跳牆了。

A3 ： I would like my mother to cook my favorite
 soup, pineapple bitter melon chicken soup.
 我想要我媽媽做我最喜歡的湯，鳳梨苦瓜雞湯。

【註】 dish〔dɪʃ〕n. 菜餚　 *fried chicken* 炸雞
　　　Buddha〔'budə〕n. 佛陀
　　　jump〔dʒʌmp〕v. 跳
　　　pineapple〔'paɪnˏæpl̩〕n. 鳳梨
　　　bitter melon 苦瓜

＊請將下列自我介紹的句子再唸一遍，請開始：

My seat number is （複試座位號碼）, and my test number
is （初試准考證號碼）.

心得筆記欄 ✏

全民英語能力分級檢定測驗

初級口說能力測驗⑤

＊請在15秒內完成並唸出下列自我介紹的句子，請開始：

My seat number is （複試座位號碼）, and my test number is （初試准考證號碼）.

I. 複誦

共五題。題目不印在試題上，經由耳機播出，每題播出兩次，兩次之間約有1~2秒的間隔。聽完兩次後，請立即複誦一次。

II. 朗讀句子及短文

共有五個句子及一篇短文，請先利用1分鐘的時間閱讀試卷上的句子與短文，然後在1分鐘內以正常的速度，清楚正確的朗讀一遍。

One　: That girl may be waiting for someone.

Two　: He has hundreds of books in his study.

Three: We have to learn these words by heart.

Four　: As soon as the thief saw me, he ran away.

Five　: I was so tired that I quickly fell asleep.

Six : Cellular phones are becoming increasingly popular. They are getting cheaper to buy and cheaper to use. They are convenient because you can get in touch with people almost anytime and anywhere. People sometimes call you, though, when you don't want to be reached. Also, some people use them in places where they disturb other people.

Ⅲ. 回答問題

共七題。題目不印在試題上,經由耳機播出,每題播出兩次,兩次之間約有 1~2 秒的間隔。聽完兩次後,請立即回答,每題回答時間 15 秒,請在作答時間內儘量的表達。

* 請將下列自我介紹的句子再唸一遍,請開始:

My seat number is <u>(複試座位號碼)</u>, and my test number is <u>(初試准考證號碼)</u>.

初級口說能力測驗⑤詳解

*請在 15 秒內完成並唸出下列自我介紹的句子，請開始：

My seat number is （複試座位號碼）, and my test number is （初試准考證號碼）.

I. 複誦

共五題。題目不印在試題上，經由耳機播出，每題播出兩次，兩次之間約有 1~2 秒的間隔。聽完兩次後，請立即複誦一次。

1. Get off the bus at the next stop.
   下一站下巴士。

2. Please help yourself to the cake.
   請自己拿蛋糕。

3. Happy birthday to you! 祝你生日快樂！

4. How are you getting along? 你過得如何？

5. Let's go fishing at the lake.
   咱們去湖邊釣魚。

【註】 *get off* 下（車）　　*help oneself to* 自行取用

　　　 get along 進展　　fish〔fɪʃ〕*v.* 釣魚

　　　 lake〔lek〕*n.* 湖

II. 朗讀句子及短文

共有五個句子及一篇短文，請先利用 1 分鐘的時間閱讀試卷上的句子與短文，然後在 1 分鐘內以正常的速度，清楚正確的朗讀一遍。

One : That girl may be waiting for someone.
那個女孩可能在等人。

Two : He has hundreds of books in his study.
他的書房裡有好幾百本書。

Three : We have to learn these words by heart.
我們必須把這些字背下來。

Four : As soon as the thief saw me, he ran away.
當小偷看到我的時候，就逃跑了。

Five : I was so tired that I quickly fell asleep.
我累得馬上就睡著了。

【註】 study〔ˋstʌdɪ〕 n. 書房
learn ~ by heart 把~背下來
as soon as 一…就~   thief〔θif〕 n. 小偷
run away 逃跑   thief〔θif〕 n. 小偷
so…that~ 如此…以致於~
tired〔taɪrd〕 adj. 疲累的   **fall asleep** 睡著

Six： Cellular phones are becoming increasingly
　　　popular. They are getting cheaper to buy and
　　　cheaper to use. They are convenient because
　　　you can get in touch with people almost anytime
　　　and anywhere. People sometimes call you,
　　　though, when you don't want to be reached.
　　　Also, some people use them in places where
　　　they disturb other people.

　　　行動電話愈來愈流行了。不論是買手機或使用手機，
　　　都比以前還要便宜。有了手機很方便，因為你可以在
　　　任何時間或地方和他人聯絡。但是，在你不想被人找
　　　到的時候，還是會有人打電話給你。而且，有人會在
　　　某些地方使用行動電話，而打擾到別人。

【註】　*cellular phone*　行動電話 (= *cell phone*)
　　　　increasingly〔ɪnˋkrisɪŋlɪ〕*adv.* 越來越
　　　　get in touch with sb. 和某人保持聯絡
　　　　though〔ðo〕*adv.* 然而
　　　　reach〔ritʃ〕*v.* 與…取得聯繫
　　　　disturb〔dɪsˋtɝb〕*v.* 打擾

Ⅲ. 回答問題

　　　共七題。題目不印在試題上，經由耳機播出，每題播出兩次，
　　　兩次之間約有 1～2 秒的間隔。聽完兩次後，請立即回答，
　　　每題回答時間 15 秒，請在作答時間內儘量的表達。

1. Q : Do you have any hobbies? What are they?
     你有嗜好嗎？是什麼嗜好？

A1 : I like to read a lot. So I consider it my hobby.
     我很喜歡閱讀。所以我認爲那是我的嗜好。

A2 : My hobby is making model airplanes. I love to look at the airplanes after I put them together.
     我的嗜好是做模型機。我最喜歡在組合完成之後，欣賞那些飛機了。

A3 : I have many hobbies. My favorite is scuba diving. Diving allows me to see the world under the sea.
     我有許多嗜好。我最喜歡水肺潛水。潛水能讓我看到海底的世界。

【註】 hobby〔'hɑbɪ〕*n.* 嗜好
     consider〔kən'sɪdə〕*v.* 認爲
     model〔'mɑdḷ〕*n.* 模型   *adj.* 用作模型的
     put~together 組合~
     scuba〔'skubə〕*n.* 水肺
     diving〔'daɪvɪŋ〕*n.* 潛水
     scuba diving 水肺潛水
     allow〔ə'laʊ〕*v.* 讓…~

2. Q　: Do you like to watch TV? Why do you like it or why don't you like it?
　　　 你喜歡看電視嗎？你為什麼喜歡或你為什麼不喜歡？

A1 : I love watching TV. I can learn what's going on around the world without ever leaving my home. Also, TV programs are very entertaining.
　　　 我喜歡看電視。我不用出門，就可以知道世界上所發生的事。而且，電視節目也很有娛樂性。

A2 : I don't like to watch TV because it's a waste of time.
　　　 我不喜歡看電視，因為很浪費時間。

A3 : I like to watch TV but I don't have time to do so. I really wish that I could have more time so I could watch TV.
　　　 我喜歡看電視，但是我沒有時間。我真的很希望我能有更多的時間，那樣我才能看電視。

【註】 *go on* 發生　　*around the world* 在全世界
　　　 entertaining〔͵ɛntɚˈtenɪŋ〕*adj.* 有娛樂性的
　　　 waste〔west〕*n.* 浪費　　wish〔wɪʃ〕*v.* 希望

3. Q : Who is your favorite singer? Why?
你最喜歡的歌手是誰？爲什麼？

A1 : My favorite singer is Celine Dion. I think she is the most beautiful person and she can sing like no one else.
我最喜歡席琳‧迪翁了。我認爲她是最美的人，而且她唱歌唱得比誰都還要好。

A2 : I like Jay the most. He is a person with a special style. I really like his style.
我最喜歡周杰倫了。他是個風格獨特的人。我眞的很喜歡他的風格。

A3 : I don't have a favorite singer because I don't listen to music.
我沒有最喜歡的歌手，因爲我不聽音樂。

---

4. Q : Do you have a pet? If you do, what is it? If you don't, what would you like to have?
你有沒有寵物？如果你有，是什麼寵物？如果沒有，你想要養什麼寵物？

【註】 *like no one else* 比誰都還要好
style〔staɪl〕*n.* 風格   pet〔pɛt〕*n.* 寵物

A1 : I have a dog and his name is Dog. I love him very much.

我有一隻狗，他的名字就叫狗。我非常愛牠。

A2 : I have a fish and I love to watch him swimming around in his tank.

我有一隻魚，我很喜歡看他在魚缸裡游來游去。

A3 : I don't have any pets, but I wouldn't mind having a pig or something.

我沒有寵物，但是我不介意養一隻像豬之類的動物。

5. Q : Your mom is going to the grocery store. You ask her to buy something for you. What would you like her to buy for you?

你媽媽要去雜貨店。你請她幫你買東西。你會請她買些什麼？

【註】 around〔əˈraʊnd〕*adv.* 到處
tank〔tæŋk〕*n.* 魚缸　　mind〔maɪnd〕*v.* 介意
or something 或什麼的
grocery〔ˈɡrosərɪ〕*n.* 食品雜貨
grocery store 雜貨店

A1 : I would like her to buy some Qoo juice for me because it is my favorite drink.

我想請她幫我買些酷果汁，因爲那是我最喜歡的飲料。

A2 : I would ask my mother to buy some watermelon. The weather is so hot and eating watermelon can cool me down.

我會請我媽媽買西瓜。天氣那麼熱，吃西瓜能使我涼爽。

6. Q : Your birthday is coming soon. What kind of presents would you like to receive?

你的生日快到了。你想收到什麼樣的生日禮物？

A1 : I would like to have a new cell phone. The phone I have now is very old and big. I want one of those small phones.

我想要有一個新手機。我現在的手機又舊又大。我要一隻那種小手機。

【註】 watermelon〔'wɔtə,mɛlən〕n. 西瓜
cool down 使涼爽　　kind〔kaɪnd〕n. 種類
receive〔rɪ'siv〕v. 收到

A2 : I want to have a new bicycle. I would be
very happy if I can have a new bicycle
on my birthday.
我想要一台新的腳踏車。如果在我生日那天，
能收到一台新的腳踏車的話，我會很開心的。

---

7. Q　: Which season do you like the most?
你最喜歡哪一個季節？

A1 : I like summer the most. I can go to the
beach and enjoy the sun during summer.
我最喜歡夏天了。在夏天，我可以去海邊
曬太陽。

A2 : I love wintertime. I love the snowy scenery
very much. Too bad we don't get snow in
Taiwan.
我最喜歡冬天了。我非常喜歡雪景。不過，
真可惜，台灣不下雪。

【註】 season〔'sizn〕n. 季節　 beach〔bitʃ〕n. 海邊
the sun 陽光　 during〔'djurɪŋ〕prep. 在…期間
wintertime〔'wɪntɚ‚taɪm〕n. 冬季
snowy〔'snoɪ〕adj. 下雪的
scenery〔'sinərɪ〕n. 風景　 ***too bad*** 真可惜

* 請將下列自我介紹的句子再唸一遍,請開始:

My seat number is <u>(複試座位號碼)</u>, and my test number
is <u>(初試准考證號碼)</u>.

全民英語能力分級檢定測驗

初級口說能力測驗⑥

*請在15秒內完成並唸出下列自我介紹的句子，請開始：

My seat number is （複試座位號碼）, and my test number is （初試准考證號碼）.

I. 複誦

共五題。題目不印在試題上，經由耳機播出，每題播出兩次，兩次之間約有 1～2 秒的間隔。聽完兩次後，請立即複誦一次。

II. 朗讀句子及短文

共有五個句子及一篇短文，請先利用 1 分鐘的時間閱讀試卷上的句子與短文，然後在 1 分鐘內以正常的速度，清楚正確的朗讀一遍。

One : That old man bought a pair of trousers yesterday.

Two : Please turn off the television.

Three: Bruce visits me from time to time.

Four : Let's go by bus instead of by train.

Five : Can you figure out how to solve this problem?

Six : National lotteries are common around the world. They originated in France as a way to make money for the king instead of raising taxes. Nowadays, people play the lottery because they dream about being rich. Even though there is only a slight chance of winning, many people still believe that one day they might be the lucky winner.

Ⅲ. 回答問題

共七題。題目不印在試題上,經由耳機播出,每題播出兩次,兩次之間約有 1~2 秒的間隔。聽完兩次後,請立即回答,每題回答時間 15 秒,請在作答時間內儘量的表達。

*請將下列自我介紹的句子再唸一遍,請開始:

My seat number is （複試座位號碼）, and my test number is （初試准考證號碼）.

初級口說能力測驗⑥詳解

*請在 15 秒內完成並唸出下列自我介紹的句子，請開始：

My seat number is （複試座位號碼）, and my test number is （初試准考證號碼）.

I. 複誦

共五題。題目不印在試題上，經由耳機播出，每題播出兩次，兩次之間約有 1～2 秒的間隔。聽完兩次後，請立即複誦一次。

1. How do you like this bag?
   你覺得這個皮包怎麼樣？

2. Say hello to your parents for me.
   幫我跟你的爸爸媽媽問好。

3. I belong to the Tennis Club. 我是網球社的。

4. Nice meeting you. 很高興能認識你。

5. My father takes a walk every day.
   我爸爸每天散步。

【註】 **say hello to** 和～打招呼；向～問好
　　　 belong to 屬於　　 tennis〔'tɛnɪs〕n. 網球
　　　 club〔klʌb〕n. 社團　 **take a walk** 散步

II. 朗讀句子及短文

共有五個句子及一篇短文，請先利用 1 分鐘的時間閱讀試卷上的句子與短文，然後在 1 分鐘內以正常的速度，清楚正確的朗讀一遍。

One : That old man bought a pair of trousers yesterday.
那位老先生昨天買了一條褲子。

Two : Please turn off the television.
請把電視關掉。

Three : Bruce visits me from time to time.
布魯斯偶爾會來拜訪我。

Four : Let's go by bus instead of by train.
我們坐巴士去，不要坐火車去。

Five : Can you figure out how to solve this problem?
你有想到要如何解決這個問題嗎？

【註】 *a pair of* 一條～　　trousers〔'traʊzɚz〕*n. pl.* 褲子
turn off 關掉（電器）　　visit〔'vɪzɪt〕*v.* 拜訪
from time to time 偶爾（= *sometimes*）
instead of 而不是　　*figure out* 想出
solve〔salv〕*v.* 解決
problem〔'prɑbləm〕*n.* 問題

Six : National lotteries are common around the world. They originated in France as a way to make money for the king instead of raising taxes. Nowadays, people play the lottery because they dream about being rich. Even though there is only a slight chance of winning, many people still believe that one day they might be the lucky winner.

全國性的獎券（樂透獎）在全世界都很普遍。獎券起源於法國，目的是為了要在不加稅的情況下，來增加國王的收入。現在，人們買獎券是因為他們做發財夢。雖然贏的機率很小，但是許多人還是相信，總有一天他們可能會成為幸運的贏家。

【註】 national〔'næʃənḷ〕adj. 全國性的
lottery〔'lɑtərɪ〕n. 獎券
common〔'kɑmən〕adj. 普遍的
around the world 在全世界
originate〔ə'rɪdʒə,net〕v. 起源
France〔fræns〕n. 法國　　way〔we〕n. 方法
raise〔rez〕v. 提高　　tax〔tæks〕n. 稅
nowadays〔'naʊə,dez〕adv. 現今
dream about 夢想；渴望
even though 儘管；即使
slight〔slaɪt〕adj. 微小的
chance〔tʃæns〕n. 機會　　win〔wɪn〕v. 贏
lucky〔'lʌkɪ〕adj. 幸運的

III. 回答問題

共七題。題目不印在試題上,經由耳機播出,每題播出兩次,
兩次之間約有 1~2 秒的間隔。聽完兩次後,請立即回答,
每題回答時間 15 秒,請在作答時間內儘量的表達。

1. Q : Do you like PE class? Why or why not?
你喜歡體育課嗎?為什麼或為什麼不?

A1 : I love PE class. We don't get to do a lot
of exercise, so PE class is the only time
for us to exercise.
我最喜歡上體育課了。我們不常做運動,所以
體育課是我們唯一能運動的時候。

A2 : I don't like PE class because doing all
those exercises makes me all sweaty
and smelly.
我不喜歡上體育課,因為做運動會讓我滿身
臭汗。

【註】 **PE** 體育 (= *physical education*)
exercise〔'ɛksə,saɪz〕*n.* 運動
get to V. 有機會做~
sweaty〔'swɛtɪ〕*adj.* 滿身大汗的
smelly〔'smɛlɪ〕*adj.* 臭的

2. Q : Describe one of your friends.

請描述一位你的朋友。

A1 : My friend Jim is a 14-year-old boy. He is
about 165 centimeters tall and he is happy
all the time.

我的朋友吉姆是個 14 歲的男生。他大概有 165
公分高，而且總是很開心。

A2 : My friend Robert is a fat pig. He never
showers and stinks all the time. He can
never do anything right. Come to think
of it, he is not really my friend. I just met
him through some misfortune.

我的朋友羅伯特是個大肥豬。他從來不洗澡，經常
發臭。他什麼事都做不好。仔細想想，他其實不
算是我的朋友。我只是倒楣認識他而已。

【註】 describe〔dɪ'skraɪb〕v. 描述
centimeter〔'sɛntə,mitɚ〕n. 公分
all the time 總是；一直
shower〔'ʃauɚ〕v. 淋浴
stink〔stɪŋk〕v. 發臭
come to think of it 仔細想想
through〔θru〕prep. 因為；由於
misfortune〔mɪs'fɔrtʃən〕n. 不幸

A3 : Kelly is my best friend. She has long hair
and a very cute smile.

凱莉是我最好的朋友。她有一頭長髮和非常
可愛的笑容。

───────〰〰〰〰───────

3. Q : In your opinion, what is your weakness?

以你的觀點來看，你的缺點是什麼？

A1 : My weakness is perhaps shyness. I am
afraid to meet new people because I am
too shy.

我的缺點也許是害羞。我不太敢去認識新朋友，
因為我太害羞了。

A2 : I like to sleep all the time. It is a weakness
I want to conquer.

我總是想睡覺。這是我想克服的缺點。

【註】 opinion〔ə'pɪnjən〕 n. 意見
in one's opinion 依某人之見
weakness〔'wiknɪs〕 n. 缺點
perhaps〔pɚ'hæps〕 adv. 或許
shyness〔'ʃaɪnɪs〕 n. 害羞
shy〔ʃaɪ〕 adj. 害羞的
conquer〔'kaŋkɚ〕 v. 克服

A3：I think my weakness is being lazy. I get lazy sometimes and I don't want to do anything.

我覺得我的缺點是懶惰。我有時會懶到什麼事都不想做。

～～～～～～～～～～

4. Q ：Describe an embarrassing experience.

請描述一次尷尬的經驗。

A1：One time I was playing basketball with my friends and one of them grabbed me by the pants. My pants were ripped and I had to wear my ripped pants all day.

有一次，我和我的朋友在打籃球，然後有人抓住我的褲子。我的褲子被扯破了，而我卻還要穿那條破褲一整天。

【註】 lazy〔'lezɪ〕adj. 懶惰的
embarrassing〔ɪm'bærəsɪŋ〕adj. 令人尷尬的
experience〔ɪk'spɪrɪəns〕n. 經驗
grab〔græb〕v. 抓住
pants〔pænts〕n. pl. 褲子
rip〔rɪp〕v. 扯破

A2： I was talking with my friends and walking at the same time and I bumped into the garbage truck and almost fell into it.

我和我的朋友一面走路，一面聊天，然後我不小心撞到垃圾車，差一點掉進去。

A3： I had to pee once. There were no restrooms anywhere. I finally decided to go behind a car to pee. I thought no one would see me but after I was done, a man in the car rolled down the window and told me that I was a bad boy for peeing on his car.

我有一次很想上廁所。到處都沒有廁所。我最後決定躲在一輛汽車後面尿尿。我以為沒人會看到我，可是在我尿完之後，車子裡有一個人把車窗搖下，對我說我是一個壞孩子，因為我尿在他的車子上。

【註】 ***bump into*** 撞上

　　　garbage〔ˋgɑrbɪdʒ〕*n.* 垃圾

　　　truck〔trʌk〕*n.* 卡車　　***garbage truck*** 垃圾車

　　　pee〔pi〕*v.* 小便　　　once〔wʌns〕*adv.* 有一次

　　　restroom〔ˋrɛst͵rum〕*n.* 廁所（= *rest room*）

　　　decide〔dɪˋsaɪd〕*v.* 決定

　　　done〔dʌn〕*adj.* 完成的　　***roll down*** 搖下

5. Q : What did you do last night?
　　　　你昨天晚上做了什麼？

A1 : I watched TV and went to bed early.
　　　　我看了電視，然後早早去睡覺。

A2 : I went to the movie theater last night. I
　　　　watched *Spider-Man*. It was a great movie.
　　　　我昨天晚上去電影院，看「蜘蛛人」。眞好看。

A3 : I went to the night market last night with
　　　　my parents. We ate a lot of food and my
　　　　parents bought me some toys.
　　　　我昨晚和我爸媽去逛夜市。我們吃了很多東西，
　　　　我爸媽還買了一些玩具給我。

6. Q : Do you buy books? What kind of books do
　　　　you like to buy?
　　　　你會買書嗎？你喜歡買什麼樣的書？

【註】　*movie theater* 電影院
　　　　spider〔'spaɪdɚ〕*n.* 蜘蛛
　　　　night market 夜市
　　　　toy〔tɔɪ〕*n.* 玩具

A1：I buy books all the time. I like to buy science fiction novels when I go to the bookstores.

我經常買書。我去書店的時候會買科幻小說。

A2：Yes, I buy books. I like to buy comic books, especially those Japanese comic books. I also like to buy books which tell historical stories.

是的，我會買書。我喜歡買漫畫書，尤其是日本漫畫。我也喜歡買講歷史故事的書。

A3：I don't buy books at all because my parents will buy whatever I want for me.

我從不買書，因爲我爸媽會買任何我想要的東西給我。

【註】　fiction〔ˈfɪkʃən〕n. 小說
science fiction 科幻小說
novel〔ˈnɑvl̩〕n. 小說
comic books 漫畫書
especially〔əˈspɛʃəlɪ〕adv. 尤其是
Japanese〔ˌdʒæpəˈniz〕adj. 日本的
historical〔hɪsˈtɔrɪkl̩〕adj. 歷史的
not…at all 一點也不…
whatever〔ˈhwɑtˈɛvɚ〕pron. 不論什麼事物

7. Q ： Do you like to go to the night market?
　　　 你喜歡去逛夜市嗎？

A1 ： I like to go to the night market a lot. You
　　　 can get anything you want there. The food
　　　 is also great.
　　　 我很喜歡去逛夜市。在夜市裡，什麼東西都能
　　　 買到。那裡的食物也不錯。

A2 ： I like to go to the night market sometimes.
　　　 I go there for special types of food I can not
　　　 get elsewhere. There are also many vendors
　　　 selling pretty trinkets.
　　　 我有時會喜歡去逛夜市。我會去那裡吃別處吃
　　　 不到的東西。那裡還有許多攤販，會賣漂亮的
　　　 小玩意。

【註】 get〔gɛt〕v. 買（= buy）
　　　 type〔taɪp〕n. 類型
　　　 elsewhere〔'ɛls͵hwɛr〕adv. 在別處
　　　 vendor〔'vɛndɚ〕n. 小販
　　　 pretty〔'prɪtɪ〕adj. 漂亮的
　　　 trinket〔'trɪŋkɪt〕n.（戴在身上的）小飾物

A3 : I don't like to go to the night market at all. It is crowded and uncomfortable. I especially hate the stinky tofu vendors. Their stalls stink so bad that I feel like throwing up every time I go near it.

我一點也不喜歡去逛夜市。夜市裡又擠又不舒服。我尤其不喜歡賣臭豆腐的攤子。那些攤子臭到，我每次靠近都會想吐。

【註】 crowded〔'kraʊdɪd〕adj. 擁擠的
uncomfortable〔ʌn'kʌmfətəbḷ〕adj. 不舒服的
hate〔het〕v. 討厭；不喜歡
stinky tofu 臭豆腐
stall〔stɔl〕n. 攤子
bad〔bæd〕adv. 非常（= *badly*）
feel like + V-ing 想要~　　　 **throw up** 嘔吐
every time 每當

* 請將下列自我介紹的句子再唸一遍，請開始：

My seat number is （複試座位號碼）, and my test number is （初試准考證號碼）.

全民英語能力分級檢定測驗

初級口說能力測驗⑦

*請在15秒內完成並唸出下列自我介紹的句子，請開始：

My seat number is （複試座位號碼）, and my test number is （初試准考證號碼）.

I. 複誦

共五題。題目不印在試題上，經由耳機播出，每題播出兩次，兩次之間約有 1～2 秒的間隔。聽完兩次後，請立即複誦一次。

II. 朗讀句子及短文

共有五個句子及一篇短文，請先利用 1 分鐘的時間閱讀試卷上的句子與短文，然後在 1 分鐘內以正常的速度，清楚正確的朗讀一遍。

One　: Who lives in that house over there?

Two　: Can you drive me to school tomorrow?

Three: I am going to visit Frank at his office.

Four　: Those people are playing basketball.

Five　: Can you hand me that dictionary over there?

Six : Johnny saw a sick puppy on his way to school one morning. He wanted to take the puppy with him, but he had to be at school. So Johnny left the puppy where he found it. After school, Johnny went back to find the puppy, but it was already gone. Johnny went home feeling sad. When he walked into the house, he saw the puppy. It turned out that Johnny's mother saw the puppy on the street and decided to adopt it.

Ⅲ. 回答問題

共七題。題目不印在試題上，經由耳機播出，每題播出兩次，兩次之間約有 1～2 秒的間隔。聽完兩次後，請立即回答，每題回答時間 15 秒，請在作答時間內儘量的表達。

* 請將下列自我介紹的句子再唸一遍，請開始：

My seat number is （複試座位號碼）, and my test number is （初試准考證號碼）.

初級口說能力測驗 ⑦ 詳解

＊請在 15 秒內完成並唸出下列自我介紹的句子，請開始：

My seat number is （複試座位號碼）, and my test number
is （初試准考證號碼）.

I. 複誦

共五題。題目不印在試題上，經由耳機播出，每題播出兩
次，兩次之間約有 1～2 秒的間隔。聽完兩次後，請立即
複誦一次。

1. I want to go see a movie. 我想去看電影。

2. What did you learn at school today?
   你今天在學校學了什麼？

3. Finish your homework quickly!
   趕快做完你的功課！

4. Do you want to play basketball? 你想要打籃球嗎？

5. Hand me that book, please. 請把那本書拿給我。

【註】 *go see a movie* 去看電影（＝ *go and see a movie*）
finish〔ˈfɪnɪʃ〕*v.* 完成
quickly〔ˈkwɪklɪ〕*adv.* 快速地
hand〔hænd〕*v.* 把…交給

II. 朗讀句子及短文

共有五個句子及一篇短文，請先利用 1 分鐘的時間閱讀試卷上的句子與短文，然後在 1 分鐘內以正常的速度，清楚正確的朗讀一遍。

One : Who lives in that house over there?
誰住在那邊的那間房子裡？

Two : Can you drive me to school tomorrow?
你明天能開車送我到學校嗎？

Three : I am going to visit Frank at his office.
我要去法蘭克的辦公室拜訪他。

Four : Those people are playing basketball.
那些人正在打籃球。

Five : Can you hand me that dictionary over there?
你可以把在那邊的字典拿給我嗎？

【註】 *over there* 在那裡　*drive sb.* 開車送某人
visit (ˈvɪzɪt) v. 拜訪　office (ˈɔfɪs) n. 辦公室
basketball (ˈbæskɪtˌbɔl) n. 籃球
dictionary (ˈdɪkʃənˌɛrɪ) n. 字典

Six：Johnny saw a sick puppy on his way to school one morning. He wanted to take the puppy with him, but he had to be at school. So Johnny left the puppy where he found it. After school, Johnny went back to find the puppy, but it was already gone. Johnny went home feeling sad. When he walked into the house, he saw the puppy. It turned out that Johnny's mother saw the puppy on the street and decided to adopt it.

某天早上，強尼上學途中，看到一隻生病的小狗。他想要把狗帶走，但是他必須到學校上課。所以強尼把小狗留在原地。放學後，強尼回去找小狗，但牠已經不見了。強尼難過地回家。當他踏入家門的時候，他看見那隻小狗。原來是強尼的媽媽在路上看到那隻小狗，然後決定收養牠。

【註】 puppy〔'pʌpɪ〕*n.* 小狗
on one's way to ~ 在某人前往~的途中
leave〔liv〕*v.* 遺留（三態變化為：leave-left-left）
gone〔gɔn〕*adj.* 消失的　　sad〔sæd〕*adj.* 悲傷的
turn out 結果是　　decide〔dɪ'saɪd〕*v.* 決定
adopt〔ə'dɑpt〕*v.* 收養

III. 回答問題

共七題。題目不印在試題上,經由耳機播出,每題播出兩次,兩次之間約有 1~2 秒的間隔。聽完兩次後,請立即回答,每題回答時間 15 秒,請在作答時間內儘量的表達。

1. Q : Have you ever been to the zoo? How did you like it?

你有去過動物園嗎?你覺得怎麼樣?

A1 : I've never been to the zoo. I'd love to go to the zoo, but I don't know how to get there. I am going to ask my mother to take me there sometime.

我從來沒去過動物園。我很想去動物園,可是我不知道要怎麼到那裡。我會要求媽媽改天帶我去那裡。

【註】 ***have been to*** 曾經去過(表經驗)

zoo〔zu〕*n.* 動物園

would love to V. 想要　　***get there*** 到那裡

ask *sb.* ***to V.*** 要求某人做~

sometime〔ˈsʌmˌtaɪm〕*adv.* 日後;改天

A2 : I love the zoo! I've been to many zoos—
some big and some small. Zoos are great.
我很喜歡動物園！我去過很多動物園。有些
很大，有些很小。動物園很棒。

2. Q : When was your birthday and how did you
celebrate it?
你的生日是在什麼時候？你是如何慶祝的？

A1 : My birthday was on February 18th. My
parents took me out for a big dinner and I
invited many friends over for a party.
我的生日是二月十八日。我爸爸媽媽會帶我
出去，吃頓豐盛的晚餐，我還邀請很多朋友
過來參加派對。

【註】 celebrate〔'sɛlə,bret〕v. 慶祝
take sb. out 帶某人出去
big〔bɪg〕adj. 豐盛的
invite〔ɪn'vaɪt〕v. 邀請
over〔'ovə〕adv. 過來

A2： My birthday was on April 1st. I did not celebrate my birthday because when I tell people about my birthday, they always think that I am playing an April Fools' joke on them.

我的生日是四月一日。我沒有慶祝生日，因為當我告訴別人我過生日，他們總是認為我是在開他們愚人節的玩笑。

A3： I don't really remember when my birthday is. We don't celebrate birthdays at home because it was the day of suffering for our mother.

我不大記得自己的生日是什麼時候。我們家裡不過生日，因為生日是母親受苦的日子。

【註】 joke〔dʒok〕n. 玩笑
play a joke on sb. 對某人開玩笑
April Fool's (*Day*) 愚人節
remember〔rɪ'mɛmbɚ〕v. 記得
suffering〔'sʌfərɪŋ〕n. 痛苦

3. Q : Do you like to live in a big city or a small
       town?
       你喜歡住在大城市或是小城鎮？

A1 : I love to live in a big city. There's everything
     in a big city. It is very convenient to live in
     a big city.
     我喜歡住在大城市。在大城市裡，東西應有盡有。
     住在大城市很方便。

A2 : I like living in a small town. Everyone
     knows each other and we all get along great.
     The sky is always clear so I can see the stars.
     The air is also fresh.
     我喜歡住在小城鎮。大家都彼此認識，而且相處
     愉快。天空總是晴朗無雲，所以我可以看到星星。
     空氣也很新鮮。

【註】 city〔'sɪtɪ〕 n. 城市　　 town〔taʊn〕 n. 城鎮
     convenient〔kən'vinjənt〕 adj. 方便的
     each other 彼此　　 *get along* 和睦相處
     great〔gret〕 adv. 很好地　　 sky〔skaɪ〕 n. 天空
     clear〔klɪr〕 adj. 晴朗的
     star〔star〕 n. 星星　　 air〔ɛr〕 n. 空氣
     fresh〔frɛʃ〕 adj. 新鮮的

4. Q : Where are you going this weekend?

你這週末要去哪裡？

A1 : I am going to the movies with my friends.

We are going to see a new action movie.

I heard it is very exciting.

我要和朋友去看電影。我們要去看一部新上映
的動作片。聽說很刺激。

A2 : I was going to go to the beach, but then I
had to come here to take this test. After
the test, I am going to the beach.

我原本要去海邊，但是後來卻必須到這裡考試。
考完試後，我要去海邊。

A3 : I'm going to visit my grandparents in Ilan.
Maybe we'll eat in a seafood restaurant to
celebrate my grandma's birthday.

我要去宜蘭探望我的祖父母。也許我們會到海鮮
餐廳吃飯，慶祝祖母的生日。

【註】 *action movie* 動作片　　hear〔hɪr〕*v.* 聽說
exciting〔ɪk'saɪtɪŋ〕*adj.* 刺激的
beach〔bitʃ〕*n.* 海灘　　test〔tɛst〕*n.* 考試
grandparents〔'grænd,pɛrənts〕*n. pl.* 祖父母
seafood〔'si,fud〕*n.* 海鮮

5. Q : Do you like trees? Why or why not?
　　　　你喜歡樹木嗎？為什麼或為什麼不？

　A1 : I love trees. I think trees are the most
　　　wonderful things in this world. People
　　　cannot live without trees.
　　　我喜歡樹木。我認為樹木是這世界上，最美
　　　好的事物。沒有樹木的話，人類無法生存。

　A2 : Trees are great and they are beautiful. I
　　　don't know what this world would be like
　　　without trees.
　　　樹木很棒，而且很美。如果沒有樹木，我不知道
　　　這個世界會變成什麼樣子。

　A3 : I like trees because green is a good color for
　　　our eyes. Besides, we can sit under a tree
　　　in the shade when it's hot.
　　　我喜歡樹木，因為綠色對我們的眼睛有益。此外，
　　　天氣炎熱的時候，我們可以坐在樹下乘涼。

　【註】 wonderful〔'wʌndəfəl〕*adj.* 美好的；很棒的
　　　　 without〔wɪð'aut〕*prep.* 沒有
　　　　 cannot live without 不能沒有
　　　　 be good for 對～有益
　　　　 besides〔bɪ'saɪdz〕*adv.* 此外
　　　　 shade〔ʃed〕*n.* 樹蔭；陰涼處

6. Q : Do you know how to ride a bicycle? If you do, how do you like it? If you don't, why not?

你知道怎麼騎腳踏車嗎?如果你會騎,你覺得怎麼樣?如果你不會騎,為什麼不會?

A1 : I know how to ride a bicycle. In fact, I love to ride bicycles. It is the best method of transportation. It is good for our health and it does not cause any pollution.

我知道如何騎腳踏車。事實上,我喜歡騎腳踏車。那是最棒的交通工具。腳踏車對我們的健康有益,而且不會造成污染。

A2 : I don't know how to ride a bicycle. I never learned how to do it. I would like to learn, though.

我不知道如何騎腳踏車。我從來沒學過如何騎腳踏車。可是我想學。

【註】 ***in fact*** 事實上   method〔'mεθəd〕*n.* 方法
transportation〔,trænspə'teʃən〕*n.* 運輸工具
health〔hɛlθ〕*n.* 健康   cause〔kɔz〕*v.* 引起
pollution〔pə'luʃən〕*n.* 污染
would like to V. 想要
though〔ðo〕*adv.* 然而(一般放在句尾)

7. Q ： What did you do last night?

你昨天晚上做了些什麼？

A1 ： I went to the cram school last night. After school, I watched some TV and went to bed early.

我昨天晚上去補習班。下課後，我看了一下電視，然後很早就上床睡覺了。

A2 ： I went to see a movie with my parents. We saw *Lord of the Rings*. It was a great movie.

我和爸爸媽媽去看電影。我們看「魔戒」。那部電影很好看。

A3 ： I had a lot of homework to do yesterday. So I was at home doing my homework all night. After I finished my homework, I went to bed.

我昨天有很多功課要做。所以我整晚都待在家裡做功課。功課做完後，我就上床睡覺了。

【註】　*cram school* 補習班　　*after school* 放學後
　　　　go to bed 上床睡覺　　lord〔lɔrd〕 *n.* 統治者
　　　　ring〔rɪŋ〕 *n.* 戒指
　　　　done〔dʌn〕 *adj.* 做完的 < *with* >

* 請將下列自我介紹的句子再唸一遍，請開始：

My seat number is （複試座位號碼）, and my test number is （初試准考證號碼）.

全民英語能力分級檢定測驗

初級口說能力測驗⑧

* 請在 15 秒內完成並唸出下列自我介紹的句子，請開始：

My seat number is （複試座位號碼）, and my test number is （初試准考證號碼）.

I. 複誦

共五題。題目不印在試題上，經由耳機播出，每題播出兩次，兩次之間約有 1～2 秒的間隔。聽完兩次後，請立即複誦一次。

II. 朗讀句子及短文

共有五個句子及一篇短文，請先利用 1 分鐘的時間閱讀試卷上的句子與短文，然後在 1 分鐘內以正常的速度，清楚正確的朗讀一遍。

One　: What are you doing this weekend?

Two　: Can you hand me that towel?

Three: That old man needs his cane.

Four　: I am going to Canada for vacation tomorrow.

Five　: Mary lost her cell phone yesterday.

Six　: Tony is a newspaper delivery boy. He has to wake up every morning at four o'clock to deliver newspapers. He gets the papers from the street corner and starts to fold them. After he folds the newspapers, he loads them onto his bicycle and starts to deliver them. He finishes at about six and then gets ready for school.

Ⅲ. 回答問題

共七題。題目不印在試題上，經由耳機播出，每題播出兩次，兩次之間約有 1～2 秒的間隔。聽完兩次後，請立即回答，每題回答時間 15 秒，請在作答時間內儘量的表達。

* 請將下列自我介紹的句子再唸一遍，請開始：

My seat number is （複試座位號碼）, and my test number is （初試准考證號碼）.

初級口說能力測驗⑧詳解

* 請在 15 秒內完成並唸出下列自我介紹的句子，請開始：

My seat number is （複試座位號碼）, and my test number is （初試准考證號碼）.

I. 複誦

共五題。題目不印在試題上，經由耳機播出，每題播出兩次，兩次之間約有 1～2 秒的間隔。聽完兩次後，請立即複誦一次。

1. Look at that puppy! 你看那隻小狗！

2. I want to use the computer. 我想用電腦。

3. Can you buy me a Coke?
   你可以幫我買一罐可樂嗎？

4. Jimmy loves to play computer games.
   吉米喜歡打電玩遊戲。

5. I forgot my key. 我忘記帶鑰匙。

【註】 puppy〔'pʌpɪ〕 n. 小狗　　use〔juz〕 v. 使用
　　　 buy sb. sth. 幫某人買某物
　　　 computer game 電玩遊戲
　　　 forget〔fɚ'gɛt〕 v. 忘記　　key〔ki〕 n. 鑰匙

II. 朗讀句子及短文

共有五個句子及一篇短文，請先利用 1 分鐘的時間閱讀試卷上的句子與短文，然後在 1 分鐘內以正常的速度，清楚正確的朗讀一遍。

One : What are you doing this weekend?
你這週末要做什麼？

Two : Can you hand me that towel?
你可不可以把那條毛巾遞給我？

Three : That old man needs his cane.
那位老人家需要柺杖。

Four : I am going to Canada for vacation tomorrow.
我明天要去加拿大度假。

Five : Mary lost her cell phone yesterday.
瑪麗昨天把她的手機弄丟了。

【註】 hand〔hænd〕v. 傳遞　　cane〔ken〕n. 柺杖
Canada〔'kænədə〕n. 加拿大
vacation〔ve'keʃən〕n. 假期
lose〔luz〕v. 遺失（三態變化為：lose-lost-lost）
cell phone 手機

Six : Tony is a newspaper delivery boy. He has to
Wake up every morning at four o'clock to deliver
newspapers. He gets the papers from the street
corner and starts to fold them. After he folds the
newspapers, he loads them onto his bicycle and
starts to deliver them. He finishes at about six
and then gets ready for school.

東尼是個送報生。他必須每天早上四點鐘起床去送報
紙。他到街角領報紙，然後開始摺報紙。摺完報紙後，
他把報紙裝到他的腳踏車上，然後開始送報。他大概
在六點鐘送完，然後準備去上學。

【註】　newspaper〔'njuz,pepɚ〕n. 報紙（= paper）

delivery〔dɪ'lɪvərɪ〕n. 遞送

wake up 醒過來；起床

deliver〔dɪ'lɪvɚ〕v. 遞送

corner〔'kɔrnɚ〕n. 街角　　start〔start〕v. 開始

fold〔fold〕v. 摺疊　　load〔lod〕v. 裝載

onto〔'antə〕prep. 到…之上

finish〔'fɪnɪʃ〕v. 完成　　then〔ðɛn〕adv. 然後

ready〔'rɛdɪ〕adj. 準備好的＜for＞

school〔skul〕n. 上學

III. 回答問題

共七題。題目不印在試題上,經由耳機播出,每題播出兩次,
兩次之間約有 1∼2 秒的間隔。聽完兩次後,請立即回答,
每題回答時間 15 秒,請在作答時間內儘量的表達。

1. Q : What do you usually do when you go home?
你回家後通常會做什麼?

A1 : I usually watch TV for an hour when I go
home. Then I will do my homework.
我回家後,通常會看電視看一個小時。然後我
會做功課。

A2 : I usually eat dinner when I get home. After
dinner, I help my mother with the dishes.
Then I watch some TV.
我回家後,通常會吃晚餐。吃晚餐後,我會幫
媽媽洗碗。然後我會看一下電視。

【註】 homework〔'hom͵wɝk〕n. 功課
help sb. with sth. 幫助某人做某事
dishes〔'dɪʃɪz〕n. pl. 碗盤

A3：I have to go to cram school after school every day, so I usually go home late.　When I get home, I am so tired that I go to bed right away.

每天放學後，我必須去補習班，所以我通常會晚回家。到家後，我太累了，所以馬上就上床睡覺。

---

2. Q　：Please give a brief description of your school.

請簡單描述你的學校。

A1：I go to a coed junior high school.　There are 35 students in my class.　There are a lot of trees at my school.

我就讀一間男女合校的國中。我們班上有三十五個學生。學校裡面有很多樹。

【註】　***cram school*** 補習班　　late〔let〕*adv.* 晚
so…that~ 如此…以致於~
tired〔taɪrd〕*adj.* 疲累的　　***right away*** 馬上
brief〔brif〕*adj.* 簡短的
description〔dɪ'skrɪpʃən〕*n.* 描述
coed〔'ko'ɛd〕*adj.* 男女合校的
junior high school 國中

A2： My school is in the mountains. It is a small
private school. I have to take a two-hour
bus ride every day. I really like my school.
我的學校在山上。那是一間小型的私立學校。
我每天必須花兩個小時坐公車。我真的很喜歡
我的學校。

A3： I go to a girls' high school. It is located
in the downtown area. There are many trees
and ponds at my school. It is also close to
my home.
我就讀一所女校。學校位於市中心。我的學校
有許多樹木和池塘。學校也離我家很近。

【註】 mountain (ˈmaʊntn̩) *n.* 山
in the mountains 在山上
private (ˈpraɪvɪt) *adj.* 私立的
ride (raɪd) *n.* 乘坐；搭乘
high school 中學
located (loˈketɪd) *adj.* 位於⋯的 < *in* >
downtown (ˌdaʊnˈtaʊn) *adj.* 市中心的
area (ˈɛrɪə) *n.* 地區　　pond (pɑnd) *n.* 池塘
close (klos) *adj.* 接近的 < *to* >

3. Q : Have you ever visited a farm? How did
     you like it? 你有去過農場嗎？覺得怎麼樣？

A1 : I went to a dairy farm last year. There were
     many cows there and we drank fresh milk.
     It was a very interesting experience. I am
     looking forward to visiting it again.
     我去年去一家乳牛牧場。那邊有很多乳牛，而
     且我們喝了新鮮的牛乳。那是個很有趣的經驗。
     我期待能夠再去一次。

A2 : I've never been to a farm before. I think it
     would be an interesting experience for a city
     boy like me. But I've also heard that it can
     be very smelly at a farm, so I am a little
     afraid of going.
     我以前從沒去過農場。我想對於一個像我這樣在
     都市長大的男孩而言，那會是個很有趣的經驗。
     但是我也聽說農場臭味很重，所以我有點害怕。

【註】 dairy〔'dɛrɪ〕 n. 酪農場 (= dairy farm)
      cow〔kaʊ〕 n. 乳牛　　fresh〔frɛʃ〕 adj. 新鮮的
      interesting〔'ɪntrɪstɪŋ〕 adj. 有趣的
      experience〔ɪk'spɪrɪəns〕 n. 經驗
      look forward to V-ing 期待
      smelly〔'smɛlɪ〕 adj. 有臭味的

4. Q : You went to the store to buy something. The clerk was supposed to give you back fifty dollars but he only gave you ten. What do you say to the clerk?

你去店家買某樣東西。店員應該找你五十元，但他卻只找你十元。你要對店員說什麼？

A1 : Excuse me, sir. You were supposed to give me fifty back but you only gave me ten. Can you give me the rest of the money?

先生，對不起。你應該找我五十元，但你只給我十元。可以把其餘的錢給我嗎？

A2 : Hey! You owe me forty dollars more. You gave me a ten-dollar coin instead of a fifty-dollar one.

嘿，你還欠我四十元。你給我一個十元硬幣，不是五十元硬幣。

【註】 clerk〔klɜk〕n. 店員
be supposed to V. 應該～　　**give back** 歸還
rest〔rɛst〕n. 其餘部分
hey〔he〕interj. 嘿（用以喚起注意等）
owe〔o〕v. 欠（錢）　　coin〔kɔɪn〕n. 硬幣
instead of 而不是

5. Q : If you were eating dinner and the power went off, what would you do?

如果你在吃晚餐的時候，停電了，你會怎麼辦？

A1 : I would try to find a flashlight or some candles so we could finish eating dinner. We would have a candlelit dinner instead.

我會試著找一支手電筒或一些蠟燭，這樣才能把晚餐吃完。我們將改吃一頓燭光晚餐。

A2 : I would try to finish my dinner in the dark and at the same time try to locate where all my favorite foods were.

我會試著在一片漆黑中把晚餐吃完，同時努力找到我最喜歡的食物擺在哪裡。

【註】 power (ˈpauɚ) n. 電力　　*go off* 停止供應

flashlight (ˈflæʃ,laɪt) n. 手電筒

candle (ˈkændl̩) n. 蠟燭

candlelit (ˈkændl̩,lɪt) adj. 燭光的

a candlelight dinner 燭光晚餐

instead (ɪnˈstɛd) adv. 作爲代替

in the dark 在黑暗中

at the same time 同時

locate (loˈket) v. 找出

favorite (ˈfevərɪt) adj. 最喜歡的

A3： I would be really scared and probably panic. I'd probably hide under the table or something.

我眞的會很害怕，可能會驚慌失措。我可能會躲在桌子下面或什麼的。

6. Q ： Do you read comic books? If you do, what is your favorite and if you don't, why not?

你喜歡看漫畫書嗎？如果你喜歡的話，你的最愛是什麼，那如果你不喜歡的話，爲什麼不呢？

A1： My favorite comic book is *Blackjack*. After reading it, I wanted to be a doctor just like him.

我最喜歡的漫畫書是「怪醫黑傑克」。看了那部漫畫後，我想成爲像他一樣的醫生。

【註】 scared〔skɛrd〕*adj.* 害怕的

probably〔'prɑbəblɪ〕*adv.* 可能

panic〔'pænɪk〕*v.* 驚慌　　hide〔haɪd〕*v.* 躲藏

or something 或什麼的

comic book 漫畫書

favorite〔'fevərɪt〕*n.* 最喜歡的人或物

　adj. 最喜歡的

A2： I read comic books. My favorite comic book
is *Sailor Moon* because she is very cute and
has magic powers.

我看漫畫書，我最喜歡的漫畫是「美少女戰士」。
因為她非常可愛，而且有魔力。

A3： I don't read comic books at all. I think it is
a waste of time and my time is too valuable
to waste.

我根本不看漫畫書。我認為那是浪費時間，而且
我的時間很寶貴，不能浪費。

7. Q ： If it were your mother's birthday, what
would you buy for your mother?

如果今天是你媽媽的生日，你會買什麼送媽媽？

【註】 sailor〔ˈselɚ〕 n. 水手　　moon〔mun〕 n. 月亮
cute〔kjut〕 adj. 可愛的
magic〔ˈmædʒɪk〕 adj. 魔法的
power〔ˈpauɚ〕 n. 力量　　*not…at all* 一點也不
waste〔west〕 n. v. 浪費
too…to V. 太…以致於不
valuable〔ˈvæljuəbl̩〕 adj. 寶貴的

A1： I would buy her a bunch of her favorite flowers and I would give it to her when everybody in the family is sitting at the dinner table.

我會買給她一束她最愛的花，然後在全家人都坐在餐桌前用餐的時候，送給她。

A2： I would buy my mother the book she has always wanted.

我會買給媽媽那本她一直想要的書。

A3： I don't have any money to buy her presents, so I would make her a birthday card. I would draw the card myself and mail it to her office.

我沒有錢買禮物送她，所以我會做一張生日卡片給她。我會自己畫卡片，然後寄到她的辦公室。

【註】 bunch〔bʌntʃ〕n.（一）束
sit at the dinner table 坐在餐桌前
present〔'prɛznt〕n. 禮物
make〔mek〕v. 做　　draw〔drɔ〕v. 畫
mail〔mel〕v. 郵寄　　office〔'ɔfɪs〕n. 辦公室

＊請將下列自我介紹的句子再唸一遍，請開始：

My seat number is （複試座位號碼）, and my test number is （初試准考證號碼）.

全民英語能力分級檢定測驗

初級口說能力測驗⑨

* 請在 15 秒內完成並唸出下列自我介紹的句子，請開始：

My seat number is （複試座位號碼）, and my test
number is （初試准考證號碼）.

I. 複誦

共五題。題目不印在試題上，經由耳機播出，每題播出兩
次，兩次之間約有 1～2 秒的間隔。聽完兩次後，請立即
複誦一次。

II. 朗讀句子及短文

共有五個句子及一篇短文，請先利用 1 分鐘的時間閱讀試
卷上的句子與短文，然後在 1 分鐘內以正常的速度，清楚
正確的朗讀一遍。

One　：This is the best restaurant in the city.

Two　：Joe is going to visit his family in New York
　　　　City.

Three：Andy went to Disneyland and had lots of fun.

Four　：I am going to buy that CD next week.

Five ： This bus is too crowded.

Six ： Vivian decided one morning to drive to work instead of taking the bus. When she arrived, she started to look for a parking spot. After circling the area several times, she still could not find a parking space. Vivian decided to go home and leave her car at home. She ended up taking the bus.

Ⅲ. 回答問題

共七題。題目不印在試題上，經由耳機播出，每題播出兩次，兩次之間約有 1～2 秒的間隔。聽完兩次後，請立即回答，每題回答時間 15 秒，請在作答時間內儘量的表達。

＊請將下列自我介紹的句子再唸一遍，請開始：

My seat number is （複試座位號碼）, and my test number is （初試准考證號碼）.

初級口說能力測驗⑨詳解

*請在 15 秒內完成並唸出下列自我介紹的句子，請開始：

My seat number is （複試座位號碼）, and my test number is （初試准考證號碼）.

I. 複誦

共五題。題目不印在試題上，經由耳機播出，每題播出兩次，兩次之間約有 1~2 秒的間隔。聽完兩次後，請立即複誦一次。

1. This TV show is funny. 這個電視節目很有趣。

2. My plant is dying. 我的植物快死了。

3. The poor puppy can't find his way home.
   那隻可憐的小狗找不到回家的路。

4. I am so thirsty. 我非常渴。

5. I am going traveling. 我要去旅行。

【註】 show〔ʃo〕n. 節目　funny〔ˋfʌnɪ〕adj. 有趣的
plant〔plænt〕n. 植物　dying〔ˋdaɪɪŋ〕adj. 垂死的
poor〔pʊr〕adj. 可憐的　puppy〔ˋpʌpɪ〕n. 小狗
so〔so〕adv. 非常（= very）
thirsty〔ˋθɝstɪ〕adj. 口渴的
travel〔ˋtrævl̩〕v. 旅行

II. 朗讀句子及短文

共有五個句子及一篇短文，請先利用 1 分鐘的時間閱讀試卷上的句子與短文，然後在 1 分鐘內以正常的速度，清楚正確的朗讀一遍。

One ： This is the best restaurant in the city.
這是這個城市最好的餐廳。

Two ： Joe is going to visit his family in New York City.
喬將去探望他在紐約市的家人。

Three ： Andy went to Disneyland and had lots of fun.
安迪去迪士尼樂園，玩得很愉快。

Four ： I am going to buy that CD next week.
我下禮拜要去買那張 CD。

Five ： This bus is too crowded.
這輛公車太擁擠了。

【註】 visit〔'vɪzɪt〕v. 拜訪；探望
family〔'fæməlɪ〕n. 家人
Disneyland〔'dɪznɪ,lænd〕n. 迪士尼樂園
have fun 玩得愉快
lots of 許多的（= a lot of）
crowded〔'kraʊdɪd〕adj. 擁擠的

Six : Vivian decided one morning to drive to work
instead of taking the bus. When she arrived, she
started to look for a parking spot. After circling
the area several times, she still could not find a
parking space. Vivian decided to go home and
leave her car at home. She ended up taking the
bus.

某天早上，薇薇安決定要開車去上班，不要坐公車。
當她到達時，就開始找停車位。在附近地區繞了好幾
圈後，她找不到停車位。薇薇安決定回家，把車子留
在家裡。反正她最後還是搭公車。

【註】　decide〔dɪ'saɪd〕v. 決定
　　　　instead of 而不是　　arrive〔ə'raɪv〕v. 到達
　　　　start〔stɑrt〕v. 開始　　*look for* 尋找
　　　　spot〔spɑt〕n. 地點
　　　　parking spot 停車位（= *parking space*）
　　　　circle〔'sɝkl̩〕v. 環繞…移動
　　　　area〔'ɛrɪə〕n. 地區　　time〔taɪm〕n. 次數
　　　　leave〔liv〕v. 遺留
　　　　end up 以…作為結束；最後

Ⅲ. 回答問題

共七題。題目不印在試題上,經由耳機播出,每題播出兩次,兩次之間約有 1~2 秒的間隔。聽完兩次後,請立即回答,每題回答時間 15 秒,請在作答時間內儘量的表達。

1. Q : Do you like to eat pizza? Why or why not?
你喜歡吃披薩嗎?為什麼或為什麼不?

A1 : I love to eat pizza. It is the greatest food ever invented. I heard that it was invented in China one thousand years ago.
我喜歡吃披薩。它是有史以來,所發明的食物中,最好吃的。我聽說,它是一千年前在中國發明的。

A2 : I don't think pizza is tasty at all. I don't like it and I don't know why so many people like to eat pizza. Pizzas are so greasy and will make people fat.
我一點都不覺得披薩好吃。我不喜歡披薩,而且不知道為什麼有這麼多人喜歡吃披薩。披薩很油膩,會讓人變胖。

【註】 pizza (ˈpitsə) *n.* 披薩
ever (ˈɛvɚ) *adv.* 有史以來
invent (ɪnˈvɛnt) *v.* 發明　　hear (hɪr) *v.* 聽說
not…at all 一點也不　　tasty (ˈtestɪ) *adj.* 好吃的
greasy (ˈgrizɪ) *adj.* 油膩的

2. Q : What is your favorite ice cream flavor?

你最喜歡的冰淇淋口味是什麼？

A1 : My favorite flavor is chocolate. I won't eat ice cream at all if the flavor isn't chocolate.

我最喜歡的口味是巧克力。冰淇淋如果不是巧克力口味的，我根本就不吃。

A2 : My favorite ice cream flavor is strawberry, especially when it is made with fresh strawberries.

我最喜歡的冰淇淋口味是草莓，特別是用新鮮草莓做出來的冰淇淋。

A3 : I don't like to eat ice cream so I don't have a favorite flavor.

我不喜歡吃冰淇淋，所以沒有特別喜歡的口味。

【註】 favorite（'fevərɪt）*adj.* 最喜愛的
ice cream 冰淇淋　　flavor（'flevə）*n.* 口味
chocolate（'tʃakəlɪt）*n.* 巧克力
strawberry（'strɔ,bɛrɪ）*n.* 草莓
especially（ə'spɛʃəlɪ）*adv.* 特別是
fresh（frɛʃ）*adj.* 新鮮的

3. Q : Do you enjoy going to baseball games?
   你喜歡去看棒球比賽嗎?

A1 : I've never been to a baseball game before.
     I've heard it is lots of fun and I sure would
     like to go check one out.
     我沒有去看過棒球比賽。聽說非常好玩,我一定
     要去瞧瞧。

A2 : I love going to baseball games. I always
     go with my father and we always have a
     lot of fun. Too bad they don't have
     baseball games all year round.
     我喜歡去看棒球比賽。我總是和爸爸一起去,
     我們都會看得很高興。真可惜,他們沒有全年
     都有棒球比賽。

~~~~~~~~~~~~~~~~~~~~~~~~~~~~~

4. Q : Do you like to go sing at a KTV?
   你喜歡去 KTV 唱歌嗎?

【註】 *have been to* 曾經去過(表經驗)
      lots of 很多的(= *a lot of*)
      fun〔fʌn〕*adj.* 好玩的   sure〔ʃur〕*adv.* 一定
      check~out 瞧一瞧~   *have fun* 玩得愉快
      too bad 真可惜   *all year round* 整年
      go sing 去唱歌(= *go and sing*)

A1 : I don't like to go to KTVs. I think it is a
waste of money. If I want to sing, I will
just stay home and sing. There really is no
need to go to a KTV.
我不喜歡去 KTV。我認為那是浪費錢。如果我想
唱歌，我會待在家裡唱。實在沒有必要去 KTV。

A2 : I love KTVs. I can go there and have my
own private concert. When I am singing
in a KTV, I feel like a superstar.
我喜歡 KTV。我可以去那裡，舉行我自己的個
人演唱會。我在 KTV 唱歌的時候，覺得自己像
是一個超級巨星。

A3 : I've never been to a KTV before so I can't
really say if I like it or not. I think I would
probably like it because I like to sing a lot.
我從來沒去過 KTV，所以我不能確定自己到底喜
不喜歡。我想我可能會喜歡，因為我很喜歡唱歌。

【註】 waste〔west〕n. 浪費　　stay〔ste〕v. 停留
own〔on〕adj. 自己的
private〔'praɪvɪt〕adj. 私人的
concert〔'kɑnsɝt〕n. 演唱會
superstar〔'supɚˏstar〕n. 超級巨星
probably〔'prɑbəblɪ〕adv. 可能

5. Q : What is your favorite juice? Why?

你最喜歡什麼果汁？為什麼？

A1 : My favorite juice is tomato juice. It is tasty and healthy. It is supposed to be full of vitamins and prevent cancer.

我最喜歡蕃茄汁。它可口又有益健康。據說蕃茄含有豐富的維他命，可以預防癌症。

A2 : I like to drink watermelon juice. It is the most refreshing juice there is. When I am thirsty, I can drink two or three cups one after another.

我喜歡喝西瓜汁。那是最清涼的果汁了。我口渴的時候，可以一次喝個兩三杯。

【註】 tomato〔təˈmeto〕n. 蕃茄

healthy〔ˈhɛlθɪ〕adj. 有益健康的

suppose〔səˈpoz〕v. 認為　　*be full of* 充滿

vitamin〔ˈvaɪtəmɪn〕n. 維他命

prevent〔prɪˈvɛnt〕v. 預防

cancer〔ˈkænsɚ〕n. 癌症

watermelon〔ˈwɔtɚˌmɛlən〕n. 西瓜

refreshing〔rɪˈfrɛʃɪŋ〕adj. 清涼的；使清爽的

句中的 there is 是用來加強語氣。

A3： My favorite juice is carrot juice. It is full of vitamins and good for my eyes. On top of that, it tastes great.

我最喜歡紅蘿蔔汁。它含有豐富的維他命，而且對眼睛有益。除此之外，味道很棒。

6. Q ： Do you watch the news on TV?

你看電視新聞嗎？

A1： I don't watch TV that much so I don't watch the news at all. When I do watch TV, I watch cartoons.

我不常看電視，所以我根本不看新聞。我要看電視的時候，就是看卡通。

【註】 carrot〔ˈkærət〕*n.* 紅蘿蔔

be good for 對…有益

on top of 除…之外（還）

taste〔test〕*v.* 嚐起來

great〔gret〕*adj.* 很棒的

news〔njuz〕*n.* 新聞

cartoon〔kɑrˈtun〕*n.* 卡通

A2 : I watch the news all the time. That is the
only way I keep myself informed of what's
going on around the world.

我總是看新聞。那是我讓自己知道全世界發生
什麼事情的唯一方法。

7. Q : What is your favorite holiday?

你最喜歡什麼節日？

A1 : My favorite holiday is Christmas. On this
day there will be people dressed up as Santa
Claus and we will get presents. It is the
happiest day of the year.

我最喜歡的節日是聖誕節。在這一天，會有人打
扮成聖誕老公公的樣子，而且我們會收到禮物。
這是一年當中最快樂的一天。

【註】 *all the time* 一直；總是   way〔we〕*n.* 方法
keep〔kip〕*v.* 使保持在…狀態
informed〔ɪnˈfɔrmd〕*adj.* 消息靈通的
go on 發生（= *happen*）
around the world 在全世界
holiday〔ˈhɑləˌde〕*v.* 節日
dress up 裝扮   *Santa Claus* 聖誕老公公

A2 : I love Chinese New Year. Everyone in
my family will gather together and
celebrate New Year. I will also get many
red envelopes.

我喜歡農曆新年。我的家庭成員會團聚在一起，
慶祝新年。我也會收到很多紅包。

【註】 **Chinese New Year** 農曆新年
gather〔'gæðɚ〕v. 聚集
celebrate〔'sɛlə,bret〕v. 慶祝
envelope〔'ɛnvə,lop〕n. 信封
red envelope 紅包

＊請將下列自我介紹的句子再唸一遍，請開始：

My seat number is （複試座位號碼）, and my test number
is （初試准考證號碼）.

心得筆記欄

全民英語能力分級檢定測驗

初級口說能力測驗⑩

*請在15秒內完成並唸出下列自我介紹的句子，請開始：

My seat number is （複試座位號碼）, and my test number is （初試准考證號碼）.

I. 複誦

共五題。題目不印在試題上，經由耳機播出，每題播出兩次，兩次之間約有1～2秒的間隔。聽完兩次後，請立即複誦一次。

II. 朗讀句子及短文

共有五個句子及一篇短文，請先利用1分鐘的時間閱讀試卷上的句子與短文，然後在1分鐘內以正常的速度，清楚正確的朗讀一遍。

One　: We need to buy a new remote control for the TV.

Two　: The refrigerator is making strange noises.

Three : That was a great movie.

Four　: What did you think of that meal we just had?

Five　：There is a sale at the department store.

Six　：Robert went to the computer store to buy a computer. He asked the clerk to help him. Robert selected a powerful computer and a big monitor to go with it. The clerk also helped Robert install different programs that Robert might need. Robert was very happy with his choice and he will have a lot of use for his new computer.

III. 回答問題

共七題。題目不印在試題上，經由耳機播出，每題播出兩次，兩次之間約有 1～2 秒的間隔。聽完兩次後，請立即回答，每題回答時間 15 秒，請在作答時間內儘量的表達。

＊請將下列自我介紹的句子再唸一遍，請開始：

My seat number is （複試座位號碼）, and my test number is （初試准考證號碼）.

初級口説能力測驗⑩詳解

* 請在 15 秒內完成並唸出下列自我介紹的句子，請開始：

My seat number is ＿（複試座位號碼）＿, and my test number is ＿（初試准考證號碼）＿.

I. 複誦

共五題。題目不印在試題上，經由耳機播出，每題播出兩次，兩次之間約有 1～2 秒的間隔。聽完兩次後，請立即複誦一次。

1. I can't go out with you.　我不能跟你出去。

2. Joe's birthday is next Monday.
   喬依的生日是下星期一。

3. The traffic on this street is light.
   這條街的交通流量很小。

4. That building is still under construction.
   那棟建築物還在興建中。

【註】　**go out** 外出　　traffic〔'træfɪk〕n. 交通流量
light〔laɪt〕adj.（數量、程度）少量的
building〔'bɪldɪŋ〕n. 建築物
construction〔kən'strʌkʃən〕n. 建造
under construction 興建中

5. I enjoy reading from time to time. 我偶爾喜歡看書。

II. 朗讀句子及短文

共有五個句子及一篇短文，請先利用 1 分鐘的時間閱讀試卷上的句子與短文，然後在 1 分鐘內以正常的速度，清楚正確的朗讀一遍。

One　：We need to buy a new remote control for the TV.
　　　我們需要買一個新的電視遙控器。

Two　：The refrigerator is making strange noises.
　　　這台冰箱發出怪聲音。

Three：That was a great movie. 那是一部很棒的電影。

Four　：What did you think of that meal we just had?
　　　你覺得我們剛才吃的那一餐如何？

【註】 *from time to time* 偶爾（＝*sometimes*）
　　　remote〔rɪˋmot〕*adj.* 遙遠的
　　　control〔kənˋtrol〕*n.* 控制
　　　remote control 遙控器
　　　refrigerator〔rɪˋfrɪdʒəˏretɚ〕*n.* 冰箱
　　　strange〔strendʒ〕*adj.* 奇怪的
　　　noise〔nɔɪz〕*n.* 聲響；噪音
　　　make a noise 發出聲響；製造噪音
　　　think of 認為　　meal〔mil〕*n.*（一）餐
　　　just〔dʒʌst〕*adv.* 剛剛　　have〔hæv〕*v.* 吃

Five　：There is a sale at the department store.
百貨公司在舉行拍賣。

Six　：Robert went to the computer store to buy a
computer. He asked the clerk to help him. Robert
selected a powerful computer and a big monitor
to go with it. The clerk also helped Robert install
different programs that Robert might need.
Robert was very happy with his choice and he
will have a lot of use for his new computer.
羅伯特去電腦行買電腦。他要求店員幫他。羅伯特選
了一台功能很強的電腦，還搭配一個很大的螢幕。店
員也幫他安裝他可能需要的各種程式。羅伯特非常滿
意自己的選擇，而且他的新電腦有非常多的用途。

【註】　sale〔sel〕n. 拍賣　　*department store* 百貨公司
computer〔kəm'pjutə〕n. 電腦
ask sb. to V. 要求某人做~　　clerk〔klɝk〕n. 店員
select〔sə'lɛkt〕v. 選擇
powerful〔'pauəfəl〕adj. 功能強的
monitor〔'manətə〕n. (電腦的) 顯示器；螢幕
go with 伴隨　　install〔ɪn'stɔl〕v. 安裝
different〔'dɪfrənt〕adj. 不同的；各種的
program〔'progræm〕n. (電腦的) 程式
happy〔'hæpɪ〕adj. 滿意的 < *with* >
choice〔tʃɔɪs〕n. 選擇；選中的東西
use〔jus〕n. 用途；功能

Ⅲ. 回答問題

共七題。題目不印在試題上，經由耳機播出，每題播出兩次，兩次之間約有 1～2 秒的間隔。聽完兩次後，請立即回答，每題回答時間 15 秒，請在作答時間內儘量的表達。

1. Q : Did you read the newspaper yesterday?
你昨天有看報紙嗎？

A1 : I read the newspaper yesterday and there wasn't much news yesterday. I was quite disappointed.
我昨天有看報紙，昨天沒什麼新聞。我相當失望。

A2 : No, I did not read the newspaper yesterday. We don't get the newspaper at home, so I usually don't read newspapers.
沒有，我昨天沒看報紙。我們家裡沒買報紙，所以我通常不看報紙。

【註】 newspaper〔'njuz,pepɚ〕*n.* 報紙
news〔njuz〕*n.* 新聞
quite〔kwaɪt〕*adv.* 相當
disappointed〔,dɪsə'pɔɪntɪd〕*adj.* 失望的
get〔gɛt〕*v.* 買（= *buy*）

A3 : I read the newspaper yesterday, but only
the comic strips.

我昨天有看報紙，但只有看連環漫畫。

～～～～～～～～～～～～

2. Q　: What do you like to do after school?

放學後，你喜歡做什麼？

A1 : I hit the cybercafe as soon as I get out of
school, so I can go online to play games
with my cyberpals.

我一出校門，就直接到網咖，因此可以上網，
和我的網友玩遊戲。

【註】 comic〔'kɑmɪk〕adj. 漫畫的
strip〔strɪp〕n. 連環漫畫
comic strip 連環漫畫　　**after school** 放學後
hit〔hɪt〕v. 到達 (= reach)
cyber-〔'saɪbɚ-〕表示「電腦的」
cafe〔kə'fe〕n. 咖啡廳
cybercafe 網路咖啡廳；網咖 (= Internet cafe)
as soon as 一…就～　　**get out of** 離開
online〔'ɑn,laɪn〕adv. 連線地；在網路上
go online 上網　　pal〔pæl〕n. 伙伴；好友
cyberpal 網友 (= Net friend)

A2： I like to go window-shopping with my
classmates. After doing that, we usually
go find something delicious to eat.
我喜歡和我的同學去逛街，看看商店櫥窗。
逛完後，我們通常會去找好吃的東西吃。

A3： I like to go home and watch TV after
school, but I never get to do that, because
I always have to go to cram schools.
我喜歡放學後回家看電視，但是我從來沒有
這麼做過，因為我總是必須去補習班。

3. Q ： Do you like to eat hamburgers? Why?
你喜歡吃漢堡嗎？為什麼？

【註】 window〔'wɪndo〕 *n.*（商店）櫥窗
go window-shopping 瀏覽商店櫥窗；逛街
go find 去找（ *= go and find* ）
delicious〔dɪ'lɪʃəs〕 *adj.* 好吃的
get to V. 有可能～；有機會～
cram school 補習班
hamburger〔'hæmbɝɡɚ〕 *n.* 漢堡（ *= burger* ）

A1 : I love burgers! I'm just crazy about
hamburgers! I could eat them every day.
They are delicious! I think they are the
best food in the world!
我很愛吃漢堡！我瘋狂喜歡漢堡！我可以每天
都吃漢堡。它們好好吃！我想漢堡是全世界最
好吃的食物！

A2 : Sometimes I do and sometimes I don't. I
prefer sandwiches to hamburgers. Chicken
and fish sandwiches taste much better than
hamburgers.
我有時候喜歡，有時候不喜歡。我比較喜歡三
明治，比較不喜歡漢堡。雞肉和魚肉三明治，
比漢堡好吃多了。

【註】 crazy〔'krezɪ〕adj. 狂熱的；著迷的 < about >
in the world 在全世界
prefer〔prɪ'fɝ〕v. 比較喜歡
prefer A *to* B 喜歡 A 甚於 B
sandwich〔'sændwɪtʃ〕n. 三明治
chicken〔'tʃɪkən〕n. 雞肉
taste〔test〕v. 嚐起來

4. Q ： Your father is going to the convenience store.
　　　　 Ask him to buy some things for you.
　　　　 你爸爸要去便利商店。請他幫你買些東西。

A1 ： Hey, Dad! I'm starving! Could you please
　　　　 pick me up an apple juice, a ham sandwich,
　　　　 and a bag of chips at the 7-11? Thanks.
　　　　 嘿，爸！我快餓死了！能不能請你在 7-11 幫我買
　　　　 蘋果汁、火腿三明治，和一包洋芋片？謝謝你。

A2 ： Dad, my pen just ran out of ink. Could you
　　　　 buy me a black ink pen at the store. A can
　　　　 of Coke would be great, too! Thanks, Dad!
　　　　 爸，我的原子筆剛好沒水了。你可不可以幫我在
　　　　 那家店裡買一枝黑色原子筆。能再買一罐可口可
　　　　 樂更好！爸，謝啦！

【註】 convenience〔kən'vinjəns〕*n.* 方便
　　　 convenience store 便利商店
　　　 hey〔he〕*interj.*（喚起注意等）嘿
　　　 starving〔'stɑrvɪŋ〕*adj.* 很餓的
　　　 pick sb. up sth. 買某物給某人（= *buy sb. sth.*）
　　　 ham〔hæm〕*n.* 火腿
　　　 chips〔tʃɪps〕*n. pl.* 洋芋片（= *potato chips*）
　　　 pen〔pɛn〕*n.* 原子筆（= *ballpoint pen*）
　　　 run out of 用完　　ink〔ɪŋk〕*n.* 墨水
　　　 can〔kæn〕*n.*（一）罐　Coke〔kok〕*n.* 可口可樂

5. Q ： Do you wear glasses? How good are your eyes?
　　　你戴眼鏡嗎？你的視力好不好？

A1 ： Yes, I wear glasses. But I am wearing contact lenses right now. I am near-sighted. My eyesight is pretty bad.
　　　有，我有戴眼鏡。但是我現在戴隱形眼鏡。我有近視。我的視力相當差。

A2 ： No, I don't wear glasses. My eyesight is perfect. Thank God, I don't need glasses.
　　　沒有，我沒有戴眼鏡。我的視力很好。謝天謝地，我不需要眼鏡。

【註】 glasses〔'glæsɪz〕n. pl. 眼鏡
　　　eyes〔aɪz〕n. pl. 眼睛；視力
　　　contact〔'kɑntækt〕adj. 接觸的
　　　lens〔lɛnz〕n. 鏡片
　　　contact lenses 隱形眼鏡（= *contacts*）
　　　right now 現在（= *now*）
　　　near-sighted〔'nɪr'saɪtɪd〕adj. 近視的
　　　eyesight〔'aɪ,saɪt〕n. 視力
　　　perfect〔'pɝfɪkt〕adj. 完美的

6. Q ： How do you feel on rainy days?

下雨天的時候，你感覺如何？

A1 : Rainy days depress me. They make me feel
gloomy and sad. I hate getting wet. I don't
like to carry an umbrella around. Rainy
days really stink!

下雨天會讓我心情不好。下雨天會讓我覺得憂鬱
而且難過。我討厭被淋濕。我不喜歡隨身帶著雨
傘。下雨天眞討厭！

【註】 rainy〔'renɪ〕*adj.* 下雨的

depress〔dɪ'prɛs〕*v.* 使沮喪

gloomy〔'glumɪ〕*adj.* 憂鬱的

sad〔sæd〕*adj.* 難過的　　hate〔het〕*v.* 討厭

wet〔wɛt〕*adj.* 濕的　　carry〔'kærɪ〕*v.* 攜帶

umbrella〔ʌm'brɛlə〕*n.* 雨傘

around〔ə'raʊnd〕*adv.* 到處

stink〔stɪŋk〕*v.* 非常討厭

A2 : I love rainy days! The air is fresh. The temperature is usually cooler. Everything seems cleaner on a rainy day. I also sleep much better on rainy days.

我很喜歡下雨天！空氣很新鮮。氣溫通常會變的比較涼快。下雨天的時候，所有的事物看起來都比較乾淨。我在下雨天的時候，也睡得比較好。

7. Q : Do you think learning English is fun? Why or why not?

你覺得學英文好玩嗎？為什麼，或為什麼不？

A1 : It's not fun at my school! I think it's very boring. I like English very much, but our learning methods really put me to sleep.

在我的學校學英文不好玩！我覺得很無聊。我非常喜歡英文，但是我們的學習方法，真的會讓我昏昏欲睡。

【註】 air〔ɛr〕*n.* 空氣　　fresh〔frɛʃ〕*adj.* 新鮮的
temperature〔'tɛmprətʃɚ〕*n.* 氣溫
cool〔kul〕*adj.* 涼快的　　seem〔sim〕*v.* 似乎
clean〔klin〕*adj.* 乾淨的　　fun〔fʌn〕*adj.* 有趣的
boring〔'borɪŋ〕*adj.* 無聊的
method〔'mɛθəd〕*n.* 方法
put sb. to sleep 使某人入睡

A2：Are you kidding me? English is wonderful!
It's my favorite subject. It's fun to learn.
It's fun to speak. It's an interesting and
useful language.

你在開玩笑嗎？英文太棒了！那是我最喜歡的
科目。學英文很好玩。說英文很有趣。英文是
個有趣又有用的語言。

【註】 kid〔kɪd〕*v.* 開～玩笑
　　　 wonderful〔'wʌndəfəl〕*adj.* 很棒的
　　　 favorite〔'fevərɪt〕*adj.* 最喜愛的
　　　 subject〔'sʌbdʒɪkt〕*n.* 科目
　　　 interesting〔'ɪntrɪstɪŋ〕*adj.* 有趣的
　　　 useful〔'jusfəl〕*adj.* 有用的
　　　 language〔'læŋgwɪdʒ〕*n.* 語言

＊請將下列自我介紹的句子再唸一遍，請開始：

My seat number is (複試座位號碼) , and my test number
is (初試准考證號碼) .

附錄

全民英語能力分級檢定測驗簡介

「全民英語能力分級檢定測驗」（General English Proficiency Test），簡稱「全民英檢」（GEPT），旨在提供我國各階段英語學習者一公平、可靠、具效度之英語能力評量工具，測驗對象包括在校學生及一般社會人士，可做為學習成果檢定、教學改進及公民營機構甄選人才等之參考。

本測驗為標準參照測驗（criterion-referenced test），參考當前我國英語教育體制，制定分級標準，整套系統共分五級——初級（Elementary）、中級（Intermediate）、中高級（High-Intermediate）、高級（Advanced）、優級（Superior）。每級訂有明確能力標準（詳見表一綜合能力說明），報考者可依英語能力選擇適當級數報考，每級均包含聽、說、讀、寫四項完整的測驗，通過所報考級數的能力標準即可取得該級的合格證書。各級命題設計均參考目前各階段英語教育之課程大綱及相關教材之內容分析，期能符合國內各階段英語教育的需求、反應本土的生活經驗與特色。

「全民英語能力檢定分級測驗」各級綜合能力說明　　《表一》

級數	綜　合　能　力		備　　註
初 級	通過初級測驗者具有基礎英語能力，能理解和使用淺易日常用語，英語能力相當於國中畢業者。	建議下列人員宜具有該級英語能力	一般行政助理、維修技術人員、百貨業、餐飲業、旅館業或觀光景點服務人員、計程車駕駛等。
中 級	通過中級測驗者具有使用簡單英語進行日常生活溝通的能力，英語能力相當於高中職畢業者。		一般行政、業務、技術、銷售人員、護理人員、旅館、飯店接待人員、總機人員、警政人員、旅遊從業人員等。
中 高 級	通過中高級測驗者英語能力逐漸成熟，應用的領域擴大，雖有錯誤，但無礙溝通，英語能力相當於大學非英語主修系所畢業者。		商務、企劃人員、祕書、工程師、研究助理、空服人員、航空機師、航管人員、海關人員、導遊、外事警政人員、新聞從業人員、資訊管理人員等。

II 初級英語口說能力測驗

級數	綜　合　能　力		備　　　　　　　　　　　註
高級	通過高級測驗者英語流利順暢，僅有少許錯誤，應用能力擴及學術或專業領域，英語能力相當於國內大學英語主修系所或曾赴英語系國家大學或研究所進修並取得學位者。	建議下列人員宜具有該級英語能力	高級商務人員、協商談判人員、英語教學人員、研究人員、翻譯人員、外交人員、國際新聞從業人員等。
優級	通過優級測驗者的英語能力接近受過高等教育之母語人士，各種場合均能使用適當策略作最有效的溝通。		專業翻譯人員、國際新聞特派人員、外交官員、協商談判主談人員等。

初級英語能力測驗簡介

I. 通過初級檢定者的英語能力

聽	説	讀	寫
能聽懂簡易的英語句子、對話及故事。	能簡單地自我介紹並以簡易英語對答；能朗讀簡易文章。	能瞭解簡易英語對話、短文、故事及書信的內容；能看懂常用的標示。	能寫簡單的英語句子及段落。

II. 測　驗　內　容

測驗項目	初　試			複　試
	聽力測驗	閱讀能力測驗	寫作能力測驗	口説能力測驗
總題數	30	35	16	18
作答時間 / 分鐘	約 20	35	40	約 10
測驗內容	看圖辨義 問答 簡短對話	詞彙和結構 段落填空 閱讀理解	單句寫作 段落寫作	複誦 朗讀句子與短文 回答問題

　　聽力及閱讀能力測驗成績採標準計分方式，60分爲平均數，滿分120分。寫作及口說能力測驗成績採整體式評分，使用級分制，分爲0～5級分，再轉換成百分制。各項成績通過標準如下：

Ⅲ. 成績計算及通過標準

初　試	通過標準 / 滿分	複　試	通過標準 / 滿分
聽力測驗 閱讀能力測驗 寫作能力測驗	80 / 120 分 80 / 120 分 70 / 100 分	口說能力測驗	80 / 100 分

Ⅳ. 口說能力測驗級分説明

評分項目（一）：發音、語調和流利度（就第一、二、三部份之整體表現評分）

級　分	説　　　　　明
5	發音、語調正確、自然，表達流利，無礙溝通。
4	發音、語調大致正確、自然，雖然有錯但不妨礙聽者的了解。表達尚稱流利，無礙溝通。
3	發音、語調時有錯誤，但仍可理解。說話速度較慢，時有停頓，但仍可溝通。
2	發音、語調常有錯誤，影響聽者的理解。說話速度慢，時常停頓，影響表達。
1	發音、語調錯誤甚多，不當停頓甚多，聽者難以理解。
0	未答或等同未答。

評分項目（二）：文法、字彙之正確性和適切性（就第三部份之表現評分）

級　分	說　　　　　　明
5	表達內容符合題目要求，能大致掌握基本語法及字彙。
4	表達內容大致符合題目要求，基本語法及字彙大致正確，但尚未能自在應用。
3	表達內容多不可解，語法常有錯誤，且字彙有限，因而阻礙表達。
2	表達內容難解，語法錯誤多，語句多呈片段，不當停頓甚多，字彙不足，表達費力。
1	幾乎無句型語法可言，字彙嚴重不足，難以表達。
0	未答或等同未答。

發音、語調和流利度部份根據第一、二、三部份之整體表現評分，文法、字彙則僅根據第三部份之表現評分，兩項仍分別給 0～5 級分，各佔 50%。

計分說明：某考生各項得分如下面表格所示：

評　分　項　目	評　分　部　份	得　分
發音、語調、流利度	第一、二、三部份	4
文法、字彙之正確性和適切性	第三部份	3

百分制總分之計算：（4+3）×10 分 = 70 分

　　凡應考且合乎規定者一律發給成績單。初試及複試各項測驗成績通過者，發給合格證書，本測驗成績紀錄保存兩年。

　　初試通過者，可於一年內單獨報考複試，得重複報考。惟複試一旦通過，即不得再報考。

　　已通過本英檢測驗初級，一年內不得再報考同級數之測驗。違反本規定報考者，其應試資格將被取消，且不退費。

（以上資料取自「全民英檢學習網站」http://www.gept.org.tw）

劉毅英文初級英檢模考班

Ⅰ. 上課時間：每週日下午1：30～5：00

Ⅱ. 上課方式：完全比照財團法人語言訓練中心所做「初級英語檢定測驗」初
試標準。分為聽力測驗、閱讀能力測驗、及寫作能力測驗三部
分。每次上課舉行70分鐘的模擬考，包含30題聽力測驗，35
題詞彙結構、段落填空、閱讀理解、及16題單句寫作、及一篇
段落寫作。考完試後立即講解，馬上釐清所有問題。

Ⅲ. 收費標準：（含代辦初級檢定考試報名及簡章費用，合計 *600* 元）

期　　數	3個月	6個月	1年保證班
週　　數	12週	24週	48週
費　　用	5800元	9800元	14800元

※ 1. 劉毅英文同學優待 *1000* 元。

　　2. 保證班若無通過，免費贈送一年課程。

Ⅳ. 報名贈書：初級英檢全套書籍

報名立刻開始背誦「初級英檢公佈字彙①－⑩」

劉毅英文‧毅志文理補習班（兒美、國中、高中、成人班、全民英檢代辦報名）

國中部：台北市重慶南路一段10號7F（火車站前‧消防隊斜對面）　☎(02)2381-3148

高中部：台北市許昌街17號6F（火車站前‧壽德大樓）　☎(02)2389-5212

初級英檢複試班

- **初檢內容**：「初級英語檢定測驗」複試項目包含：
  ① 複誦。
  ② 朗讀句子與短文。
  ③ 回答問題。

- **招生目的**：協助同學通過「初級英語檢定複試測驗」。

- **招生對象**：針對已通過初級英檢初試測驗者，具有基礎英語聽力及口說能力者。

- **收費標準**：*4800* 元 (劉毅英文家教班學生學費優待 *1000* 元)

- **上課內容**：完全比照財團法人語言訓練中心所做「初級英語檢定測驗」複試標準。訓練方式分為複誦、朗讀句子與短文，回答問題三部分。每次上課前先舉行英文口說能力及聽力測驗。測驗後老師立即糾正同學的發音，並傳授正音技巧。

劉毅英文家教班 (國一、國二、國三、高一、高二、高三班)

班址：台北市重慶南路一段 10 號 7F (火車站前·日盛銀行樓上)

電話：(02) 2381-3148·2331-8822　　網址：www.learnschool.com.tw

國中九年級基本學力測驗模考班

I. **招生對象**：全國國中九年級學生

II. **開課班級**：

【全科資優班】

堂 次	上 課 時 間	週 六	上 課 時 間	週 日
第一堂	9：00～12：00	-----	9：00～12：30	數學資優班
第二堂	2：00～ 5：00	英文資優班	2：00～ 5：30	文科A班
第三堂	6：00～ 9：30	自然資優班	6：20～ 9：20	全科戰鬥營

【全科精修班】

堂 次	上 課 時 間	週 六	上 課 時 間	週 日
第一堂	9：00～12：30	數學精修班	9：00～12：30	-----
第二堂	1：30～ 5：00	自然精修班	2：00～ 5：00	文科B班
第三堂	6：00～ 9：00	英文精修班	6：20～ 9：20	全科戰鬥營

【單科班】

上 課 時 間	週 六	上 課 時 間	週 日	上 課 時 間	週 日
9：00～12：00	英文A班	9：00～12：00	英文B班	9：00～12：30	自然A班
1：30～ 5：00	數學A班	2：00～ 5：30	文科A班	2：00～ 5：30	文科B班

III. **獎學金制度**：

    1. 本班同學在學校班上，國三上學期總成績，只要有一次第一名者，可獲得獎學金*3000*元，第二名*1000*元，第三名*1000*元。

    2. 學校模擬考試，只要有一次班上前五名，可得獎學金*1000*元。

    3. 每次來本班考模擬考試，考得好有獎，進步也有獎，各種獎勵很多。

IV. **授課內容**：

    1. 本班獨創**模擬考**制度。

        根據「基本學力測驗」最新命題趨勢，蒐集命題委員參考資料，完全比照學力測驗題型編排。「基本學力測驗」得高分的秘訣，就是：**模擬考試➡上課檢討➡針對弱點加以加強**。

    2. 本班掌握最新命題趨勢：題型全為單一選擇題、題材以多樣化及實用性為原則。英文科加考書信、時刻表等題型；數學科則著重觀念題型，須建立基本觀念，融會貫通；理化科著重於實驗及原理運用。我們聘請知名高中學校老師（如建中、北一女、師大附中、中山、成功等），**完全按照基本學力測驗的題型命題**。

    3. 每週上課前先考50分鐘模擬考，考後老師立即講解，馬上釐清同學錯誤的觀念。當天考卷改完，立即發還。

劉毅英文・毅志文理補習班（兒美、國中、高中、成人班、全民英檢中心）

國中部：台北市重慶南路一段10號7F(消防隊斜對面)　☎(02)2381-3148・2331-8822

高中部：台北市許昌街17號6F(壽德大樓)　☎(02)2389-5212

||||||||||||●學習出版公司門市部●|||||||||||||||

台北地區：台北市許昌街 10 號 2 樓　TEL：(02)2331-4060・2331-9209

台中地區：台中市綠川東街 32 號 8 樓 23 室

　　　　　TEL：(04)2223-2838

|||||||||||||||||||||||||||||||||||||||||||||||||||

初級英語口說能力測驗

主　　　編 / 石 支 齊

發 行 所 / 學習出版有限公司　　　　☎ (02) 2704-5525

郵 撥 帳 號 / 0512727-2 學習出版社帳戶

登 記 證 / 局版台業 2179 號

印 刷 所 / 裕強彩色印刷有限公司

台 北 門 市 / 台北市許昌街 10 號 2 F　　☎ (02) 2331-4060・2331-9209

台 中 門 市 / 台中市綠川東街 32 號 8 F 23 室　　☎ (04) 2223-2838

台灣總經銷 / 紅螞蟻圖書有限公司　　☎ (02) 2795-3656

美國總經銷 / Evergreen Book Store　　☎ (818) 2813622

本公司網址　www.learnbook.com.tw

電 子 郵 件　learnbook@learnbook.com.tw

售價：新台幣一百五十元正

2005 年 8 月 1 日一版二刷